Lock Down Publications and Ca$h
Presents

I0664141

FRESH
OFF DA
PORCH 3

Slippaz Don't Count

Written By

IRA B.

First Edition 2025

Printed in the United States of America

This is a work of fiction. Names, characters, places, and incidents either are products of the author's imagination or are used fictitiously. Any similarity to actual events or locales or persons, living or dead, is entirely coincidental.

Lock Down Publications
P.O. Box 944
Stockbridge, GA 30281
www.lockdownpublications.com

Like our page on Facebook: Lock Down Publications
www.facebook.com/lockdownpublications.ldp

Stay Connected with Us!

Text **LOCKDOWN** to 22828 to stay up-to-date with new releases, sneak peaks, contests and more…

Like our page on Facebook:
Lock Down Publications

Join Lock Down Publications/The New Era Reading Group

Visit our website:
www.lockdownpublications.com

Follow us on Instagram:
Lock Down Publications

Email Us: We want to hear from you!

Dedication

I dedicate this book to the young niggaz who's lookin' from the front porch. Stay where you're at and find another solution. The game ain't what it used to be. there's no loyalty and integrity out there in them streetz. Don't be no fool. Be smart. Be strong. Be careful.

Chapter 1

As she ran, Dez had tears in her eyes. Rod was right behind her, moving as fast as he could. Dez was a decorated track and field athlete back in school before the streets. She kept herself in shape for such purposes as this. The person she was chasing after was quick on his feet too. But Dez was fast enough to keep him in her sights.

They'd been running for about fourteen minutes now, and Rod was heavily winded. Dez was about ten yards ahead of him and refused to let off for fear of losing her target. This was the one that shot her sister, Jazz. When Dez saw this – her sister dropping from that gunshot to the chest – she set her sights on her killer.

The chase led them through a series of paths between industrial buildings, into a nearby neighborhood, and now down a side street that her man was growing tired of running down. The target kept gazing behind him and damn near tripping over his own feet in the process. Then, his desperation to get lost led him up the steps of a residence where he burst through the front door of the house to get inside.

Bad move, Dez though because she knew she could trap him there.

"You go round back!" Dez hollered back over her shoulder at Rod, who then cut across a neighbor's front yard.

Suddenly, there were gunshots ringing out inside the house up ahead, and there was more than just one gun shooting. Dez had been gripping her gun throughout the

5

whole journey and was now curling her finger around the trigger. Then, to her astonishment, her man came backpedaling out the front door, busting his gun. Someone was forcing him back outside with hot slugs of their own. The menacing look on Dez's face told it all.

She was several yards away from her target when Dez upped her weapon and squeezed the trigger. The first shot missed, but the second one tore into his rib cage area and knocked him off his feet. Dez rushed in and stood over him. No words were needed for what she intended to do.

Blocka! Blocka! Blocka! Blocka!

As he closed in on the scene, Rod watched as the man's face exploded under the brutal assault of Dez's bullets. You could actually see bone fragments and flesh shooting up in the air from the slug's impact. Dez stared down at what used to be the killer's face.

"Wish I can wake his bitch ass up and kill him again," she replied lowly.

Then, just to emphasize her point, Dez dumped two more slugs into his chest where his heart was.

"That's enough," another voice said in their proximity.

Both Dez and Rod looked up to see two niggaz coming down the front steps of the house. Dez knew one of them as Big Head, one of Stucky Street's hustlas and a serious nigga.

"You know who this muthafucka is?" asked Big Head, coming to rest before Dez and Rod.

"All I know is he just killed my sista."

"Jazz?"

Dez nodded gravely. "Yeah."

"That's Lil One from over on Holton Street," said the other guy with bushy eyebrows and gold teeth. "He's one of them STB niggaz. I know this because my baby mama little brotha is down wit' them niggaz."

"Then that's who we take it to," said Big Head. "But for now, we need to get off the scene. Them crackaz gon' be here any minute now, and there's one more dead in the house," he added.

"Who?" Dez asked.

"My cousin, Murk," said Big Head.

That was when Rod saw it, the darkening of Dez's shirt that looked like blood drenching. Rod stepped over and moved her arm aside to get a good look at the area.

"Are you hit, Dez?" he asked.

When Dez gazed down at her side, it was then that she finally registered she'd been injured. Then, Rod lifted her shirt to inspect the injury. It left them all shocked. There, above her right hip bone, was a bullet wound the size of a quarter.

"Oh, shit," muttered Big Head.

Rod cursed under his breath. "This is bad."

And then, Dez suddenly collapsed. Instantly, Rod caught her in his arms and feared the worst. Dez had been shot and didn't even know it. This was bad indeed. Very bad.

***

All it took was for Ray to review his wife's dead body to bring that beast out of him. Then, once he reviewed the hospital's outside camera footages, although he had already known it was Von's work, what shocked him also was the fact that Tami had been in the car too. From what he could see from the video, he knew Tami had taken a shot at Von from inside the car. Von was injured, and that gave Ray some hope of catching her. Maybe the injury would slow her down enough for him to catch up to her somehow.

To find Vontoria Roberts and slaughter her whole existence was the ultimate plan. So, to keep his colleagues from reviewing the video footage and getting in his way, Ray took the footage and left the hospital. He drove himself home where he unlocked his arsenal gun cabinet to prepare for war. Ray wasn't there ten minutes before the front door opened and shut. Ray stepped to the doorway of the study office where his arsenal was hidden behind his award collection wall in a secret panel.

Entering the house was his daughter led by his former partner and good friend, Frank Grant. When the two met one another's gaze, Ray could see that Frank was both saddened and angry, but it was the sorrowful look Rayneshia was presenting that sent him moving in her direction.

"Get away from me!" Rayneshia sneered at her father, her teary eyes ablaze. "Don't fuckin' touch me, nigga. Ever! I hate you!" she screamed at him.

Right then, the front door opened, and Qay stepped into the house. He went straight for his woman and draped an arm around her shoulders that were weighted down with grief. Ray felt his hands clench into fists when he saw Qay kiss her on the cheek. Then, he led Rayneshia to her bedroom and shut the door behind them.

Frank, who was obviously troubled by what he'd just witnessed, sat down on the arm of the living room sofa. He then reached into his coat pocket for the pack of cigarettes he had there. He shook one out and offered Ray, who he knew had quit smoking ten years ago, one. But Ray accepted one instead, and Frank lit his first, knowing Ray needed it more than he did.

"You're in some deep waters, Ray," said Frank. "But I'm sure you already know this, brotha."

Ray didn't reply.

"Chief Moore has lost his cool, the whole department is concerned about you, and some even want to teach you a lesson or two as well."

"That's already happened, Frank," said Ray.

"Oh. By who?" Frank took a short drag from his cigarette and watched his friend.

He told Frank about his encounter with Lynn McKinney and her partner earlier, right after the chief chastised him in his own home.

"Now, Latrice is gone, and so is everything else, Frank. I don't got nothing left – everythang's gone!"

"Not everythang, my friend."

Ray didn't even acknowledge him.

"You don't wanna have that kinda state of mind, Ray. I know you hurtin', brotha. I know what you going through right now."

"You can't know what the hell I'm going through," Ray snapped.

"I lost my wife too, Ray. Don't you remember?"

Ray froze. "I remember," he whispered.

"Simone's been gone twelve years now. And her killer... He could just as well be any of those knuckleheads out there. But I got through it, Ray. Even after I did lose everything in the process. If it wasn't for you and the few other guys, I'd be dead or in prison right now. Now, the roles have turned, and I'm here to save you from the same fate I was facing."

"I'm good."

"Stubbornness and pride will be your downfall."

"I've already fallen, Frank."

"Yeah. With you interfering in a criminal investigation by obstructing justice by stealing evidence from the crime scene, that is enough to make you fall hard and not get back up again for a very long time, Ray." Frank stood up to face him. "Where is the video tape, Ray?"

No answer.

"Help me help you, brotha. The cat is out the bag, and before long, the chief will send a whole taskforce team to come retrieve you and that tape."

"Let them bring their ass here if they want to." Ray turned away from his friend and marched back down the hallway to his home office.

By the time Frank made it there, Ray was removing a SCAR 16S rifle from the gun rack he had installed behind the wall of his award collection. Ray set the weapon aside and reached for the M90 machine gun and cradled it in his arms for a brief moment.

"So, you're going at it alone?" asked Frank.

"You of all people know how serious I am about Von and wantin' to end her," Ray replied.

"So, she was in that video you took?"

Ray turned away from him.

"Yes. She was in the video. Seeing Remmy dead out there, I shoulda known," said Frank.

"I'm going rogue, Frank."

"I see that, brotha."

Ray said, "The only way to get Von where I want her is to play by her rules of the streets. All I need you to do is stall the other guys as long as you can. There's no other way to go about doing it except by the law of the streets."

There was no reply from Frank.

"I need to do this, Frank."

"I know."

"Now please leave and lemme do this my way. I love you, brotha," he smiled.

For a long minute, Frank didn't answer, then he nodded his head and said, "Likewise, Ray. Be careful out there. I'ma do my part."

There was nothing else Ray needed to say further. He resumed his task of preparing for a showdown. It wasn't long after Frank finally left did something else click on in Ray's mind. He stopped what he was doing and exited the room. Moments later, Ray was standing outside Rayneshia's bedroom door. He knocked and waited. When Qay opened the door, Ray beckoned him to step out, and he did.

"What?" he replied.

Ray gave him a straight-face. "How about you and me go out there right now and bury some niggaz?' he asked.

"You and me?" Qay pointed to himself.

"If I stand any chance in this family, then you know what needs to be done. You down or what?" Ray was dead serious, and there was no denying the murderousness shining in the detective's eyes.

Nothing mattered at that point but vengeance.

Retaliation was a must.

It was murder.

Chapter 2

"AP," said Rikah, brushing by Tuk and Daisy to come stand before the leader of the Gangsta Disciples. "You and us all are lookin' for the same bitch. But as of right now, you need to tell your guys to stand down. This is my family you see in this room, and they feel threatened, so I suggest that you respect my wishes." She held his gaze.

"Stand down, my Gs," AP said to his guys.

The armed guys lowered their weapons and slowly put them away, but not Twan, who was feeling some type of way. He was clutching his banger and glaring darkly at AP and his crew.

"Now tell your boy to do the same," AP stated firmly.

"Twan. Humble yourself. It's all good," said Rikah, snatching Twan out of the dark place he was in.

Reluctantly, Twan tucked his gun behind him at the waist beneath his shirt. "Make that be the last time you disrespect me and my loved ones. I don't care who you is. That shit ain't gon' slide," he said.

Rikah saw that AP was about to respond and held her hand up to silence him. Her and AP had history, and he knew better than to test her patience.

"If we stand to make this shit work, then we gon' have to work together as a team," said Rikah.

AP replied and gestured toward Daisy. "But she ain't part of the team. She rolls wit' Von and that clown ass nigga, Remmy," he snarled.

"Remmy is dead," Tami spoke up and exchanged a look with Daisy. "I did the world a favor and took his black ass out. I shot Von too, but the bitch still managed to get away," she said.

"That's bullshit," said G-Mack, the GD at the leader's right side. "You killed Remmy?" he chuckled.

"It's confirmed that Remmy is dead," said Rikah.

Then, she went on to share with AP and his guys what all had taken place down in Quincy where Von was concerned and what they already had planned for her.

"Didn't know she had no jit," said AP.

"As we all did," said BJ. Then, he moved over to stand in front of Daisy protectively. "But as for this one right here, I'll handle her myself."

Having exercised her patience long enough, Tami made it be known that she wanted the room cleared out. She wanted them all to leave and go do what it was that they needed to do, so she could be with Bebop and not disturb him from his rest.

After another minute of reaching a mutual agreement, it was then that Tami learned why AP and his guys had shown up. They had learned of Tyler McKenzie's murder and found out that it was Von who had done it. Ty was a Gangsta Disciple, and he was one of G-Mack's closest guys. So, now Von was wanted by the second most dangerous gangs in the streets. The room cleared out, leaving Tami and Twan in the room to speak amongst themselves.

"Who is really running the show, Antwan?" asked Tami, leaning against the far wall next to the door.

"No one is above the other, Tami. We all in this shit together. Our only objective is to find Von and kill her," Twan replied with a stern expression.

"But do you believe she'll sacrifice herself?"

Twan shrugged. "I don't know."

"Is she really that heartless, Antwan?"

He nodded.

With a shake of her head, Tami asked Twan if he would send someone to watch over her and Bebop. He nodded and pulled out his phone to do just that. But then, the door opened and in walked Faye, her big brother, Andre, and his son, Quick. When Tami saw her, she frowned upon the other woman.

"Rontay had to be flown out here to see another specialist," said Faye. "I saw Daisy outside, and she told me you was in here."

"Aren't you supposed to be wit' Rontay right now though, Faye? It's risky leaving him alone after all that's been going on out there in them streets."

"He wit' two reliable people."

"Who?"

"The county police," said Faye.

Tami was reminded of Rontay's participation in Manda's assault and the death of her partner. It wouldn't be long before some real heavy hitters showed up and squeezed all the information they could out of Rontay. They would see how gangsta he really was when those crackaz started naming football numbers. Shit was certainly about to get hectic. Would Rontay break?

***

As soon as the words left Cody's mouth, Teddy dropped his head wearily. Then, all of a sudden, Cody's head was snapping back from the blow of his brother's fist. Then, Teddy was all over him at once, blinded by rage and the hurt Cody caused him with his truth – the truth about killing Bizkit.

Teddy didn't see that one coming, and Bizkit was another person he looked up to. When Cody said what he said, all Teddy knew was to strike out. Now, there they were, fighting like enemies, tearing the living room up, creating a serious problem for Avery, who stood there watching in absolute astonishment. Avery didn't know what to do as he watched his two best friends battle it out in front of him.

But that was until Money Mel entered through the front door and couldn't believe his eyes. Then, he cast Avery a stern look, admonishing his silence before rushing forward to separate the other two.

"Y'all chill the fuck out!" said Money Mel.

By this time, Po' Boy and Avery had to help pull the two apart after Felicia's failure to do so, but that was when things really got cruel for them. The instant Teddy was separated from his brother, he reached a hand up to his face where two of his wounds had been broken open during the fight. His hand came back bloody, and the sight of blood seemed to fuel Teddy's rage.

"Baby, no!" Felicia screamed when she saw Teddy reach for his gun.

Instantly, Cody looked up and saw his brother pointing the gun at him. He ducked just in time as the gun exploded. The bullet missed him by a foot and slammed into the wall behind them.

"Cody, go!" Avery shouted at Cody.

"Lil brah."

Money Mel rushed in to restrain Teddy to prevent him from pulling the trigger again. He and his brother tussled with the gun for a moment while Avery and Po' Boy hurried Cody out the front door.

Shequita rushed to the front room almost naked and still dripping from the shower water. She was in her panties and a long T-shirt, showing off her fit physique and thick, brown, tattooed thighs and legs. When she laid eyes on her two sons tussling with one another and knocking over what was left from the first confrontation, Shequita stepped forward and grabbed a hold of both of them.

"The fuck is wrong wit' y'all?" Shequita demanded, seeing all the blood dripping from her youngest son's face. "Stop it now!" she shouted.

At his mother's words, Teddy allowed his brother to take the gun away. Then, he shoved Money Mel away from him and stalked toward the front door.

"Can't let you do that, Teddy," said Felicia. She had peeped the move and stood in front of the closed door to block his path from leaving.

"What's going on?" asked Shequita.

"Move outta my way, Mama Licia!" Teddy growled at Felicia, but his disdain didn't move her. "He killed my cousin," said Teddy; his rage so profound it had tears spilling from his eyes down his bloody face.

"Who killed who?" Shequita was lost.

"Cody killed Bizkit," said Money Mel.

"What!" both Shequita and Felicia replied simultaneously.

"Now, I'ma kill his muthafuckin' ass."

"No, baby. That's your brotha," Felicia said to him.

"Fuck that nigga!" Teddy turned away from her and moved toward the back of the house. "He ain't my muthafuckin' brotha!" he screamed in outrage.

Shequita lifted her hands up to her head in a what-the-fuck expression and looked at Money Mel for more clarification. He told her the truth about Bizkit's murder, not wanting to lie to his mother about something so serious.

"Damn," sighed Felicia as she moved over to sit down on the sofa chair to rest her nerves.

When it was reported that Bizkit was killed along with the others, those who knew him personally assumed someone else had done it. Cody was putting in work; did they know he had it in him? Knowing that Cody was the actual killer of some of the street's most loved and respected niggaz was shocking. Shequita was totally baffled about it.

"Oh, Cody," Shequita groaned.

Then, she headed toward Teddy's bedroom, but Teddy wasn't there at all. He'd pulled another fast one. This time, his actions were going to cause him more trouble than he could get out of. Teddy was not himself but worse, and that was enough to worry about.

Shequita came rushing back to the front room where Felicia and her oldest son were talking.

"Teddy's gone," she said.

She looked very scared.

"Gone where?"

"Out the back door," she said.

Instantly, Money Mel brushed past his mother, moving for the back door. Felicia shot up to her feet and approached her sista with a worried look on her face. Shequita was shaking so bad; she looked scared at that moment.

"You don't think he's gone after Cody again, do you?" Felicia asked.

Shequita shuddered. "I hope not."

"Should we call Tami?"

Hesitantly, Shequita shook her head and said, "Let's hope that we can straighten this mess out first."

"Hope," said Felicia. "All we can do is hope for the better."

Chapter 3

When Von exited the bathroom, she was no longer the same person she was before she went in. Von was about to do what a lot of niggaz had done before – sacrifice herself for someone she loved. Her son. The reality of her decision had reached its level of unavoidable.

Yellow was waiting for her outside of the bathroom door, and his heart tightened with the loss. He knew what was about to transpire, and he couldn't do a damn thing about it. She was about to die. The inevitable.

"We gon' take the car that's in the garage," said Yellow with a heavy heart.

In his hand were the car keys of a waiting Lexus Jeep parked off the kitchen exit.

Von said, "I gotta do this alone, Yellow. This is my decision alone, my life. But you must promise me one thang, boo." She saw the pain in his eyes no matter how much he tried to hide it.

If things were different, maybe she would have had Yellow as her nigga. His love for her was deep, and Yellow showed it in the way he made love to her. It hurt to know what she was losing in Yellow. He was a solid, young nigga. Even her man, Isaiah, approved of him.

"I already know," said Yellow. "Make sure baby boy gets out alive and get him somewhere safe."

"And if he don't?"

"Fuck all them muthafuckas whole world up," he replied with a menacing voice. Yellow reached for her hand, and Von pulled her hand away, shaking her head.

"No more of that, Yellow. Let's go." Von stepped around him and moved toward the garage door through the quiet kitchen. The room began to permeate of the death they would be leaving behind.

Yellow followed, and together, they got into the Jeep and activated the garage door by the press of a button. A minute later, they were rolling down the driveway. So far, no one had alerted the authorities of the gunshots or else a clean getaway would be impossible because those crackaz would have had the whole spot surrounded.

Once in traffic, Von told Yellow to take her to the Dungeon. He would drop her off outside and leave her at once. Yellow didn't argue with her; he just remained reverently silent because he was afraid that if he did say anything, it would put them at odds. He was hurting inside. The woman he loved was about to die, and he was taking her to meet death.

This was not like something they would read in urban books. Two lovers alongside one another, going to war with their enemies. It was some Bonnie and Clyde type shit, but this wasn't that scenario. It was plain surrender, a shocking truth compared to the caliber of individual Von was.

In the process, Von told him to seek and kill Daisy for her betrayal. She even provided him with the keys to her empire and what he needed to be her successful successor if he made it out alive, everything from her business establishments to her connections and some other thiings that she warned Yellow to cherish with his life.

As he drove, Yellow fought back the tears that threatened to break free. He wanted so badly to try and talk her out of it, but Von was being the true mother that she was. To give her life for her child's was the most honorable thing a mother could do for her son.

At the location, Yellow pulled the Jeep up at the curb outside the Dungeon. Crawfordville Highway was busy with traffic at this time of day, and its residence sat back off from the main road about thirty yards. From the road, Von could see a black vehicle parked out front in the gravel driveway. The car belonged to Ernest "Cowboy" Thorton, an affluent lawyer that Rikah somehow managed to manipulate into her game plan.

"Hold on." Yellow reached out to grab her arm before she could open the door and get out.

"You agreed…" she said.

"I know," Yellow cut her off.

He stared deeply in her eyes.

"I know you gon' do what you do anyway, but after this, I'ma leave the game alone. I'm done. Fuck all this shit, Von," he said. "I'ma take Shyleek far away from here and raise him myself."

"But what about TJ?" she asked. "And Eboni?"

It took a minute for Yellow to answer the question, and when he did, it shocked Von.

"I'ma take her too and give Shyleek a sista. Mama is a fuckin' crackhead, and I don't want baby gurl around that shit no more. I can do it. I can handle it. You got my word that I'll do right by your son and give him the life he deserves, Von. I love you, and I will continue to love you through him. I swear," he replied.

Hearing those words touched Von deeply. The tears in her eyes were evidence of how she felt.

"I love you too, Yellow."

Von reached over to hug him and kiss his cheek. Then, she pulled away from him and got out the Jeep without a backward glance. Watching her walk away from him, Yellow felt a stab of pain in his heart with every step that distanced her from him. Before he allowed himself to go after her, he put the truck in drive and sped away.

Von, with her head held high and proud, walked up the long driveway toward the Dungeon. It was almost over. When she finally made it to the house and knocked on the front door, Von knew her mother and Reyzyne were no longer there. The cleanup crew had disposed of their bodies by now. The car parked out front was a black Mercedes Benz, which was owned by Cowboy. This was one of the lawyer's three homes.

The door opened, and Cowboy Thorton stood there in his crisp button down and loose silk tie.

"Von," he replied, a man of medium height and weight, wavy, black hair, and very intense black eyes.

Von had no words for him. She drew her weapon and put a bullet through his handsome face. She entered through the door, stepping on top of his body like he was a floor rug. Leaving the front door open, Von traversed over the house to check and see if anybody else was inside. That was when she found the young white girl hiding in the bathroom, cowering behind the door. She was half naked, and Von just stared at her, empty of emotions.

"P-Please don't h-hurt me," the girl cried.

Von shot her twice in the chest and the head. Then, she walked back up front to where she retrieved her cell phone to call her enemy.

"You got some nerve callin' my fuckin' phone, Vontoria," said Rikah aggressively.

"I'm at the Dungeon," she said.

"What?"

Von sneered. "You heard what the fuck I said, bitch. I'm here," she said and disconnected. Then, she moved over to the sofa to await the arrival of her death. It was that easy, but then again, it was never that easy.

***

Avery had remained beside Cody all the way until they made it to his house like before, but this time, Cody sat down on the porch steps instead of going inside. You could tell he was filled with burning rage because he was pouring in sweat. He was even shaking, as if fighting that inner beast that was banging against the cage of his insanity. Avery looked at his brother and knew he was really hurting inside.

What just happened back at the house was a whole other situation where the other wanted to kill his brother. Teddy really wanted to murder Cody, and Cody saw the truth of the matter in his eyes. There was pure hate in them. Dark malice.

When Cody thought about his brother, his last vision of him reminded him of a monster.

"He's just mad right now about Bizkit," said Avery, leaning against the porch banister. "He knows how Bizkit was, plus he got Mel there to explain it to him in his way. Brah will see it more clearer then that you was in a dark place, and you was not in your right mind."

Cody didn't want to talk about it. For some reason, he began to think about this situation in reference to Daisy and Von's situation. Would Teddy go to the ends to try and hurt him through those he loved most?

"No," said Avery, as if reading his mind. "I know what you thinking, brah. Brah loves you. We are family. He's just mad and hurtin' right now. The last thang he'll want to do is hurt us to get at you for that stupid shit."

"How you do that, Av?" he asked.

"What?"

Cody said, "Always seems to know what I'm thinkin'?" He reached to stroke his throbbing jaw where Teddy rocked him with one of his heavy fists.

Little big brotha hit hard.

When Avery opened his mouth to speak, he was interrupted by the lone car that came to a halt behind him at the curb. Avery turned toward the bluish four-door car with the dark tinted windows. Behind him, Cody stood up and stared at the vehicle, but not without removing the gun from his waistband. He was ready for the fuckery.

"You know who that is?" Avery asked.

"I seen that car before…" Cody paused when the passenger door opened, and Stefani Daniels got out and circled around the car. By this time, the driver and rear passenger doors opened, and Pumpkin Jones and Mya Bates climbed out behind one another, but it was Stefani that held the attention of Cody. It had nothing to do with how pretty she was.

Avery glanced back at Cody and smirked mischievously.

"What you grinning for, Av?" he questioned.

"Your girlfriend came to check up on you."

"Stefani's not my girlfriend."

"Then what is she, brah?" Avery persisted.

"Av," Cody called him.

"Huh?"

"Shut up." Cody felt butterflies fluttering in his stomach, as he watched Stefani and her friends approach.

Not wanting to make Stefani feel uncomfortable with the gun, he tucked it back at his waist. Stefani led the way, and when she was in arm's reach, she pulled Cody into her embrace. By his own accord, Cody hugged her back while inhaling her sweet scent and the strawberry shampoo in her hair.

"You okay, Cody?" Stefani asked.

"No."

"Yeah. That was a stupid question," she said. Then, she stepped back to look at him. "I thought it was good to stop and check on you. I heard about what's all been happening wit' you lately," said Stefani.

"Depends on what you've heard," Avery stated.

"The same thang the streets are saying," Mya responded. Her brother, Stix, was an official street dude who lived out in Mt. Pleasant.

Mya was Stefani's closest friend next to Pumpkin, who'd just joined the circle.

"Sometimes, the streets overexaggerates thangs," Cody replied without blinking.

"And I'm BooBoo tha Fool." Stefani frowned, her light brown eyes alight with emotion. "Can I talk to you one on one for a minute, Cody?" she asked.

Cody couldn't deny her even if he tried. He nodded, and Stefani took him by the hand like it was the normal thing to do. Then, together, they entered the house through the front door. This would be the first time Stefani had been in his house. She immediately sensed the death in the air the moment she walked through the door. Cody didn't take her any farther than the living room, but she began pacing the floor at once. Stefani had gone total flip mode in the blink of an eye. When Cody saw this, he immediately became concerned because of her actions. Stefani looked worried.

"What's wrong, Stefani?" he asked.

She stopped pacing and turned her gaze on him. This time, when their eyes met, Cody saw fear in them.

"I got something to tell you," she said.

"Just say it."

"Okay." She paused briefly. "They're saying you killed Dred," replied Stefani.

Cody looked at her intensely.

"He was my big brotha," Stefani cried.

That was when Cody felt a spark somewhere near his heart. The truth read in his eyes, and there was no way he could look at Stefani and deny its truth. Then, the totally unexpected happened.

Chapter 4

When Aunt Pooh looked up at the entrance at her boss, Keith Holland, she automatically knew something serious was amiss. Although the man had a habit of carrying a grave expression, the look on his face at that moment was worrisome. Pooh had a feeling he was about to say some wicked shit.

There were four others in the lounge room of the workplace, and they all turned up their noses at Keith's presence. Obviously, no one liked him, and Keith knew this, which was why he never let off on giving them hell. The man was a nuisance, a fuckin' asshole.

"What have I done now, Holland?" said Pooh, standing next to her friend and work buddy, Samantha, in front of the coffee machine.

Keith was a large man of about six-foot-four and nearly three hundred pounds. His presence seemed to fill the whole room and take away most of its air, or maybe his total existence made it difficult for the others wanting to breathe in the same air as him.

"What makes you think you've done something, Reynolds?" said Keith, referring to Pooh by her former name of her late husband and the same name that was still documented in her files.

"Because I'm the only person you've been lookin' at since you walked through the door," said Pooh.

"Reynolds, how many times I've voiced to you about bringing trouble to this school?"

"Again, what have I done?"

"Well, apparently, it's not me this time you have to worry about," said Keith. "There's a police detective here to see you about an issue."

"A detective?" Samantha looked over at Pooh worriedly, her sharp chin quivering under her astonishment.

When Pooh heard this, the first thing that came to her mind was Von, and her heart gripped with dread. But first, she had to make sure the detective was actually who he said he was. You couldn't be too careful when there was a war out there, and everybody was a potential target. Pooh placed her coffee mug on the counter between her and Samantha. Then, she headed for the door.

En route to the administrator's building, Pooh questioned Keith about the detective's identity.

"Detective Ray Williams is what he said his name was," Keith told her, as they walked side by side down the hallway, headed toward his office.

Detective Ray Williams. The name registered immediately the instant it came out of his mouth. Pooh knew the man only by reputation. He had cornered her a few times – once in regard to the vendetta he had with Von some time ago. She would never forget a man like Ray; he was determined and powerful in a way that couldn't be denied.

"Is this about that niece of yours, Reynolds?" Keith felt the need to ask because when Von herself attended the school, she was more than a handful.

He was aware of Von's street reputation and thought Pooh was partially to blame for how Von turned out.

"I don't know anything, Keith," she replied.

"The typical answer from the auntie of a gangster."

Pooh ignored him the rest of the way, and when she finally laid eyes on Ray, she knew why he had come. She saw it in his eyes; it was written all over his face. The second she walked through the door into Ray's path, she knew her niece was no longer in the land of the living.

"Can you come wit' me downtown?" asked Ray.

"Why?" She didn't budge.

Ray shoved his hands into his pants pockets and let out a troubled sigh.

"She's dead, Pooh," he replied. "We need you to come identify the body. You're the only next of kin we can reach."

"What about my sista?" asked Pooh.

She was hoping that he could give her some clarity on her sister's whereabouts.

"She's nowhere to be found. Some of my guys are tryna track her down right now. It's been said she hasn't been in the company of her husband for hours. I'm sure that's not like your sista, eh?"

"No." Pooh shook her head and closed her eyes for a brief moment.

"Is everything alright?" Keith came over after watching them from across the room.

Pooh opened her eyes and swayed on her feet. Then, she looked at her boss, told him that she had to leave, turned away from him, and headed for the exit. When Ray saw this, a wicked smile appeared on his face as he followed her out the door. If only Pooh knew the hell she was about to walk into.

As they made their way to the parking lot, Ray told her about Von's death. He said that she had shot it out with the authorities during a high-speed chase that led to her car losing control and wrecking out. Von was currently at the county morgue awaiting identification from her next of kin. Hearing of Von's death didn't hit Pooh as hard as it would have if she hadn't already accepted the fact that her death was certain with the lifestyle she lived. It was a certainty that Pooh had already prepared herself for when that time came. Von knew she would die in the streets. It was her dream, her story.

But it was several feet away from the school where the vehicle sat with its trunk partially shut and awaiting Pooh's body while Qay waited behind the wheel when trouble came. It came in the form of a Chevy Suburban truck that stopped damn near a foot from running both of them over where they stood. Then, two armed men jumped from the SUV, carrying pistols and grim looks on their faces.

"Shit," Ray cursed when he saw Chad and Leo move in for the kill.

Pooh braced herself for the assault.

"You knew this was coming to you, Ray," said Chad, and Leo rushed him at once, bashing him in the face with his gun.

The blow's impact knocked Ray against Pooh, as she reached out to keep them both from falling on the ground. That was when Qay jumped from the car with his gun blazing. Leo was the first to catch one of the slugs with his mouth before another one struck him in the ear.

"Muthafucker!" Ray reached for his sidearm to lay Chad down, but Qay was already punching him in the chest with another hollow point bullet from his .45 caliber.

He dropped Chad, but Chad's large frame consumed the slug and refused to die. He was struggling to crawl away when Ray forced a foot in the middle of his back and said, "Look what you made me do, Chad."

Boom!

Ray's .44 Bulldog exploded and sent the back of Chad's head splattering the earth around them. Several feet away, Pooh stood there, shocked in place, still as stone, but not for long.

"It's not safe for you here," said Ray.

"Me? But they came for you, Ray," Pooh replied, as she watched blood run down Ray's face from the wound Leo caused him a minute ago.

Without further ado, Ray took her by the back of her neck and forced her into the trunk of the car. Then, they got the hell out of dodge.

***

A total of seven vehicles turned into the long driveway headed toward the Dungeon's premises. One after the other, vehicles parked, and at least two dozen goons got out packing heavy artillery. In a systematic formation, a team of shooters circled around the Dungeon with their weapons ready. Another team entered through the front door of the house. Several more went around back of the already surrounded house.

Rikah was already standing outside the SUV that she arrived in. Accompanying her was Twan and Tuk and Dutch, who had arrived at the hospital moments after AP and Rikah parted ways.

A minute after G-Mack and the others entered the house, G-Mack stepped back out on the doorstep to beckon them over. Rikah and Dutch looked at one another, and Dutch nodded grimly before leading the way forward.

"Believe it or not, the bitch done really did it," G-Mack replied, standing in the doorway where a dead body laid just behind him in the corridor.

Rikah didn't even react when she recognized the dead body that belonged to Cowboy. She stepped around him, through the entrance hall, and turned into the spacious living room where Von sat surrounded by certified killers. Von was literally sitting on the sofa, smoking a blunt and looking relaxed, as if she was not faced with sure death at that moment. At the sight of her, Twan's fists clenched tightly, and Rikah smiled like she'd won a prize.

"I only have one condition," said Von, staring up at Rikah with a serious expression. "Let my son live, Rikah."

"Don't you know you're not in the position to make demands, nor suggestions for that matter?" asked Rikah.

"You're a woman of integrity, right? Regardless of what we done been through out there in them trenches, your respect for me is undeniable."

Rikah shrugged. "If you say so."

"You got what you want, Rikah. Hey, Twan." Von saluted him in greeting, and Twan nodded grimly. "I'm ready for this shit, y'all. Let's get to it."

"This is too easy, Vontoria,' said G-Mack. "What else you got up your sleeve?"

"Nothing."

"I don't believe that for one second. The Von I know wouldn't lay down without a fight," said G-Mack.

"Then that goes to show that you don't know me at all. Because you'd know I take family matters seriously, that I'll burn the whole world down if it meant getting revenge on those who hurt them."

"Then why sacrifice your own mama and your girl instead of yourself earlier?"

Von didn't answer but held Rikah's steady gaze.

"You love your child more. That's understandable." Rikah eased closer to Von and then moved over to sit down next to her. She was far from worried about whether she was placing herself in grave danger. Von wouldn't try anything stupid; she wanted her son safe and unscratched.

"Where is Daisy?" Von asked.

"Around."

Von nodded. "You raised a solid bitch in her, Rikah."

"It runs in the family."

"What's wit' all this fuckin' chitchat shit?' snapped G-Mack, his pistol drawn and his poise threatening. "Let's kill this bitch and be done wit' it!"

That was when Von rose up to her feet to face him, and G-Mack actually stepped back.

"You wouldn't even have the nuts to kill me if you wasn't surrounded by your people. You and I both know this a fact. I own you, nigga, so let's not get it twisted."

"Fuck you, bitch!" he glared.

Von smirked. "You the bitch, nigga."

"I should…"

"Ricardo Mullens. Look it up, y'all. This bitch ass nigga turned state evidence on his own family to save himself. Then had him killed..." Von saw the blow coming and weaved G-Mack's right jab, spun alongside of him, and rocked him with a vicious hook to the jaw.

At once, two of the goons pounced on Von and were beating her ass something fierce before Rikah told them to halt, and they backed off. Von was bloody but seemed unfazed toward her beatdown and got back up on her feet to face her adversaries. G-Mack aimed his pistol at her face.

"Chill." Twan shoved his arm away, and three of G-Mack's GD brethren instantly reacted and used force to restrain him. At the same time, two of Twan and Rikah's men stepped in to counteract the GDs' efforts.

"Back the fuck off!" said Tuk, challenging one of the GDs who looked like he wanted to try something.

A shoving match ensued between another GD member and Twan before Twan forced his Glock into his cheek and was about to squeeze the trigger before a hand rested upon his shoulder. It was Von who suddenly appeared at his side, and Twan looked at her sternly.

"This my show," said Von. "You muthafuckas got my son. Y'all trippin right now. Kill me and get it over with. The longer y'all bullshit around, the longer my son is in the clutches."

Suddenly, Von materialized with her Beretta and put the gun to her own head.

"You niggaz act like y'all scared to kill a bitch!"

Rikah looked on in silent intrigue that Von had had a weapon the entire time and could have easily taken her out the game.

"This that gangsta shit right here," said Von.

"Pull that muthafucker then," said G-Mack, ready to be done with all the theatrics.

"Say no more," Von said while looking Twan dead in the eyes. He opened his mouth as if to say something, but no words came out.

Boc!

Gasps and stunned expressions traveled around the room, as Von killed herself right there in front of them all. She blew her own brains out. That was what procrastination would get you every time. While they were bullshittin' around, Von thought it best to take matters in her own hands. Von's fearlessness made her who she was. She lived by the gun.

"She went out like a fuckin' coward," said one of the younger GDs who went by the name Tec.

"Naw," said Twan. "One thang Von wasn't was a coward. That bitch was a beast," he said.

Chapter 5

It wouldn't be the first time he snuck through the back door of his house. Teddy didn't want to be around anybody. He was furious with Cody but even more with everybody because they all knew what had happened to Bizkit and failed to tell him. Bizkit was more like a brother to him than a cousin. It was he who initially introduced Teddy to the street lifestyle.

Teddy remembered that day like it was yesterday. He was walking home from school one afternoon when Bizkit pulled over alongside the road to scoop him up. Teddy was ten years old, a fifth grader. Money Mel was doing time in his juvenile program then.

"I missed the bus," said Teddy when Bizkit asked him why he was walking in the cold.

"How you missed the bus, lil cuz?"

"I had to get my radio back from Ms. Taylor." Teddy went on to explain how his tape cassette player ended up in his homeroom teacher's file cabinet.

He had stolen Money Mel's All Eyez On Me cassette tape and took it to school with him. During recess, he was on the school's playground with the other school kids, holding a cypher while rapping 2-Pac's lyrics out loud. Ms. Taylor observed the group of hyped school kids and came over and overheard Teddy's usage of profanity and promoting a revolution against the oppressors.

"I had to get Mel's tape back," said Teddy.

33

So, after school, he snuck back in his homeroom classroom and stole the tape player back from the file cabinet. By the time he made it to the bus terminal, his bus had already left the school.

"So, you decided to walk home?" said Bizkit.

Teddy shrugged. "Yeah."

"I woulda made Ms. Taylor drive me home if it had been me," Bizkit added while dumping his blunt's ashes into the empty soda can in the cup holder.

It was during that hour when Teddy smoked weed for the first time. Then, Bizkit drove him around town while he visited a couple of his dawgs and one of his side chicks. That was where Teddy saw for the first time with his own eyes just how dangerous Bizkit was.

"I know this pussy nigga ain't still coming round here after I done…" Bizkit didn't finish his words of expression and swung the Delta 88 to the curb outside of Shayla Butler's house in Shaw Quarters.

Sitting in the passenger seat, Teddy watched as his cousin reached beneath the driver's seat for the 9mm he had hidden there. Bizkit cocked the gun back and told Teddy not to get out the car. Then, he got out and marched right into the house.

A minute later, the front door opened and out stumbled another nigga bleeding from his face and holding his shoulder as if it had been dislocated. That was when Bizkit rushed after him and began pistol whippin' him in the front yard. Seeing this made Teddy get out of the car, so he could observe the situation closer.

"Stop, Bizkit!" said Shayla from the doorway of the house. "You gon' kill him, bae. Don't kill my brotha!" she cried out in fear for her brother's life.

The nigga Bizkit was tearing a new asshole was Marco, a muthafucker Bizkit despised greatly ever since he found out that Marco was bullying his sister and taking away the stuff and product Shayla would hold for Bizkit. He had been waiting to confront Marco, but Marco knew it was best to avoid Bizkit and not give him a shot at him. Marco was good at discretion – until this day. Bizkit happened to stop by the house, and Marco was there. Prior to this occurrence, Bizkit had sent word to Marco on two occasions through the grapevine, and Marco's response was aggressive, and it activated the animal in Bizkit.

Teddy learned a valuable lesson that day. That day, Mel was a fool for his baby brother, and Teddy knew this. It scared him to see Teddy smoking weed, running errands for the street hustlaz, and just being the young knucklehead that he was.

Throughout the years when Money Mel wasn't there, there was always Bizkit, and Teddy would always remember that for as long as he lived. Bizkit was aggravating at times, but what big brother wasn't? And now, Cody had killed him, and Teddy wanted so badly to hurt him severely for it – brother or not. Cody knew how close he was to Bizkit, and Teddy felt betrayed by his brother. Betrayal was unacceptable in his book.

Having distanced himself from the house and all the bullshit he left behind, Teddy had taken the back path behind his house. Fifteen minutes later, after unconsciously journeying through the neighborhood aimlessly, Teddy suddenly registered that he had brought himself to where Bizkit lived in the dead end down from Betsey Funeral Home. He stared at Ms. Ann's old house that Bizkit had renovated and made into his own domain. His beloved boxed Chevy Caprice Classic was parked in the driveway up ahead, its candy apple red paint shining beautifully as well as the twenty-eight-inch chrome face rims that had the car sitting up high and proud.

Teddy moved forward and circled the Chevy slowly, remembering the times he and Bizkit shared rolling through the streets in it and capturing all the attention. That was when the front door of the house opened, and Teddy looked up toward it. At the sight of the woman standing there, staring out after him, Teddy somehow figured this moment was already destined. He was meant to be here now.

"I'm glad you here, Teddy," said Chastidy, the only woman next to his Auntie Gina that Bizkit trusted beyond measure.

Chastidy was Bizkit's wifey, and she too was a bitch of fearlessness. When she beckoned Teddy over, he didn't even hesitate moving in her direction.

"You got a serious mission ahead of you, Teddy," she replied when Teddy came to rest in front of her.

"What mission?" he asked.

"The one your cousin wasn't able to accomplish before your brotha killed him." Chastidy scowled darkly, her yellow-bone complexion darkening with pain and rage.

Cody. Teddy couldn't think about his cousin without Cody dominating his mental visual. He wanted to wipe that vision away from his brain, to destroy everything Cody could possibly hold dear.

He entered through the door into the house. From there, there was no turning back. Whatever it was that Bizkit had left him to do, he would see that it got done – no matter what. He would become Bizkit reincarnated.

***

Luckily for Dez, the wound was through and through, and no important organs were damaged. Rod and Big Head saw that she was properly tended to by Big Head's people, who was a local veterinarian and whose medical experience was enough to save Dez from further damage.

Rod was standing outside the vet on the phone when Big Head exited through the door. The two men met for the first time outside his home where his cousin was murdered by Lil One. Together, they loaded Dez up in Big Head's dead cousin, Murk's car and drove her four blocks over to the vet.

Emmanuel, who was an associate of Big Head through his sister, Angie, was administering surgery on a German Shepherd when they came calling on his assistance. He abandoned the dog and jumped to the task of taking care of Dez.

Rod had phoned Sand to come out and see to Dez's situation on his behalf. She was on the way with her loyal assistant. Doughboy, the other guy who was occupying the house with Big Head when the shit went down, was left back at the house to situate things. He, Big Head, and Murk had just gotten back in town from Gainesville and were setting up shop to conduct their business when Lil One invaded their world. Apparently, Lil One had seen Murk entering the house moments before he decided to take advantage of the situation presented to him. Both Big Head and Doughboy were in the kitchen, breaking down a bundle of molly and designer weed, when all hell broke loose. Right after the shit went down and Dez was taken away, Doughboy went about his business of ridding the house of all the drugs and other illegals.

By now, the whole crime scene was crawling with people while Big Head and Rod watched over Dez. She was heavily medicated right now, and even while she was down, Dez was still being stubborn.

"Everythang copasetic, my man?" asked Big Head.

The name fit him perfectly because the nigga had a head so big that he couldn't have had a natural birth. Rod turned his gaze on him.

"It is what it is, homie. How 'bout your end?" he asked.

"So far so good."

"Think that shit gon' affect what you got going on?"

Rod knew he was going through it about his cousin being killed earlier. Big Head was one of the humble types, never allowing himself to get out of character, but you could tell he was hurting though.

"I'm tight wit' Lil One's old man, Preacher. We used to run in the same circle before the Feds got ahold of him four years ago."

"So, this shit will affect you then?"

"It is what it is," said Big Head. "Lil One disrespected my home; he killed my cousin in the process. He got exactly what he deserved. But my question to you is why would he be involved in your beef wit' him?"

Rod didn't want to go into details about why all this shit was happening, but he felt as though he owed Big Head at least an explanation of truth. So, he gave him a small portion on the situation where Big Head could fill in the blanks with his own perspective.

"So, this pretty much all Remmy's doing?" asked Big Head.

A woman with a dog kennel removed herself from a truck and was approaching the entrance to the vet. The cell phone in Rod's hand vibrated with an incoming call, and he saw that it was Twan.

He answered and said, "What it do?"

"It's done, my nigga," said Twan.

"What's done, brah?"

"You know who," Twan replied.

Then, Twan told him through code language of Von summoning them all to the Dungeon only to shoot herself in the head.

"Damn," Rod responded with a heavy sigh.

Twan continued on to say that Rikah had ordered the release of the child, and that was being handled at that very moment while Daisy's man, BJ, contacted his people.

From next to him, Big Head said, "One time!"

Sure enough, a police wide bodied cruiser was turning into the entrance of the plaza where the vet was located. It angled in their direction, and Big Head began to walk away from Rod up the walkway leading toward the adult X-Mark Sex Shop store to their left. Rod watched the cop car come closer while still holding the phone against his ear. He remained calm as if the presence of the cop car approaching wasn't a big deal. But Rod was strapped with his banger and knew if pressured, it could go down right there. The police cruiser curved around to circle the parking area of the plaza of stores and such. It didn't dare come Rod's way but moved in the opposite direction from which Big Head had gone.

"Why you so quiet, brah?" Twan asked.

Rod told him.

"Where is Dez?"

Twan was sure to be worried once he knew what had happened to Dez. So, Rod told him what went down, and Twan could only let out a few expressed curse words.

"Sand is on the way to check up on thangs. I thought I should call her to come over because her work is all we know," said Rod.

"You right, my nigga."

Rod watched as Big Head ducked off into the sex shop, and the police cruiser stopped right in front of it. He could have just run back inside the vet but didn't want to bring unnecessary attention on Dez. Rod had no choice but to respect that move. Next, Rod ended the call with Twan, ensuring him that he would take control of the matter. Then, he disappeared back inside the vet where he found Emmanuel in his office, scratching his head pensively.

Rod leaned against the office door jamb with a direct side view of the front entrance. Across the hall behind him, the veterinarian's assistant was tending to a middle-aged white woman and her animal. Rod could hear the woman's panicky words of concern resounding from beyond the door inside.

"You don't look so good, my brotha," Rod said to the Black man behind the cluttered desk.

Looking up at Rod with weary eyes, Emmanuel said, "I don't like this situation. It's dangerous, ya know? I've never done anything like this before. I can't let this affect my business here."

"You don't have nothing to worry about," Rod told him in a calm voice. "I appreciate what you did to help my homie back there," said Rod.

"It's all good. I just don't like being put on the spot like that. There's no tellin' how many people witnessed y'all rushin' Deziseree in here," stressed Emmanuel.

There was no reply from Rod. They really did cause a scene when they brought Dez in unexpectedly. Two customers had fled the vet's lobby when Dez came through the spot. Either one of them could have alerted the authorities of what they saw. So far, the law hadn't crashed the spot.

"If anything, you can just say I forced you under gunpoint to do it. That way, you'll be clear and keep your license," suggested Rod, and the other man looked even more alarmed by it.

"That would be unnecessary," said Emmanuel. "My Uncle Willie works for TPD as a police captain, and he would work it all out."

"If anythang ever comes of it though."

The man nodded. "Most certainly, and I know Dez. I woulda done it without hesitation anyway."

Right then, Rod got a call from Sand informing him that she'd arrived. When he stepped out to meet her, Rod was surprised to see that Twan had managed to make his presence known.

"My nigga," said Rod when he and Twan eventually met up and embraced one another. This was his nigga for real, his brother, his number one friend and confidant.

"Thank you for showing up too, sis," Rod said to Sand before bumping fists with her.

She reminded him that this was what she did best and then headed off to meet with Emmanuel to talk work.

Alone now to speak with Twan more privately, Rod then stressed the ordeal regarding Souljah's demise. A lot of bullshit was sure to come of that one too.

"I've spoken wit' Roe already," said Twan.

"What he say?"

"That we better get his man for killin' his nephew. I told him you was seeing to that already. Then, on the way here, I informed Roe that the mission is completed," Twan said.

He clapped him on the back of the shoulder and left Rod to go see Dez. That would do her some good. Jazz was gone… But she still had Twan to keep her going.

Chapter 6

Cody had just heard what he didn't expect to hear, and now, he felt conflicted. Then, Stefani threw herself into his arms and sobbed miserably. This caught Cody off guard, and Stefani was squeezing so tight that he felt like he was trapped in a vise grip. Then, that was when something moved out of the corner of Cody's eye, and he turned in its direction. That was where he spotted somebody running from the kitchen up the hallway for the back of the house.

"Move!" Cody forced Stefani's arms away from him and took off running after the person who had no business in his house.

It was a female that was taking flight. Cody chased her up the hall where she reached to snatch the back door open. She did just that and was moving over the threshold when Cody dived forward and tackled her down to the floor of the back porch. She yelped loudly, and Cody felt a jolt in his shoulder.

"Don't do it, Young C!" a voice shouted.

Cody recognized the voice before looking up to see Menace hurrying over from next door. He was moving in one of those slow, injured hurries that made him look so awkward doing so. Beneath him, the woman ranted and raved at Cody to get off of her. Cody had drawn his gun during the chase and was pressing it against the woman's head when he was stopped.

Menace said, "Don't shoot that one, lil brah. That's your family. That's Daisy's old girl," he paused before the porch steps to catch his breath.

Looking down at the female underneath him, Cody took a long, good look at her and gasped. He frowned when he recognized Kim and roughly pushed up off of her. Mad as fire, Cody didn't even bother to lend her a hand to assist her.

Avery came rushing around the back of the house with his gun out and ready. He saw Kim picking herself up off the floor and rushed forward to help her stand firmly. Then, he cast a questioning glance over at his brother, and Cody just frowned deeply.

"What's going on, Ms. Kim?" demanded Menace, easing down onto the top of the porch step.

He was hurting, but Menace was too prideful to complain.

"What you doing in my house?" Cody sized his older cousin up like he would an opponent.

"I came for your mama," said Kim.

"My mama? For what?"

She told him about what took place at the hospital earlier and then Tami's call asking her to retrieve something for her.

"What?" asked Cody, still frowning. "What my mama wanted you to come get?"

"I didn't get the opportunity to get it and find out what it is," she said.

"But why did you run?"

"Because," said Kim, "I was told of your latest escapades and didn't wanna be another one of your victims. I only came here to do what Tami asked and return it to her – whateva it is," she told him.

"Where is it?" he asked.

"In the kitchen."

"Show me."

Cody gestured toward the open back door where Stefani was standing. She turned aside to allow Daisy's mother to enter. With a shake of the head, Kim moved past her and went into the house. Cody followed closely behind her, meeting Stefani's intense gaze in passing. He could see she was dying inside. When it rained, it poured.

If it wasn't one thing, it was another, and Cody felt like he was trapped in a maze of afflictions. They wondered why he was going the fuck off, why every little thing was motivation to bring out the beast in him.

Kim led the way to the kitchen where she approached the refrigerator and opened it.

"She said for me to pull out the vegetable drawer on the bottom on the right. It should be underneath it, she said," Kim explained.

"Aight." Cody nudged her aside to kneel before the vegetable bin at the bottom.

He pulled it out, and to Cody's surprise, there was a rectangular panel that outlined its secret compartment. Cody used a finger to wedge the panel up, and there was a black, leather fanny pack tucked down inside.

"I guess that's it," said Kim.

Also crowding the space of the kitchen was Stefani and her friends, Avery and Menace, and Cody asked them all to leave except Kim. They all respected his call and exited the kitchen without complaint.

"Now, let's see what this is," said Cody.

He carried the fanny pack over to the kitchen counter where he unzipped the pack. Then, he proceeded to dump out its contents, and instantly, Kim shook her head in displeasure. What was contained in the pack was five thick rolls of rubber banded cash, multiple packages of molly, and a Zip-Loc bag that contained pieces of jewelry. There was also a brown leather wallet inside, and Cody opened it up to look inside.

"Rodney Wells," Kim read the name on the driver license inside.

Cody heard the tone in which Kim used and looked over at her questioningly.

"Who is Rodney Wells?"

She gave him a sullen look. "He's way before you even came into existence, honey."

"Who the fuck is he, Kim?" he snapped.

Startled by his aggressive tone of voice, Kim regarded Cody in a silent caution.

"About twenty years ago, Rodney was brutally murdered in his home. Somebody had slit his throat and stabbed him in the heart. Your mama was messing wit' Rodney on the side; they were what they now call friends wit' benefits."

"Who killed him, Kim?"

She shrugged.

"Who fuckin' killed him? Because it doesn't look right that my mama still carrying around this man's wallet after he's been dead all these years," said Cody. "I'm not stupid, Kim, so don't try to play me."

"I'm not trying to play you, Cody. Ask your mama what happened to Rodney. Only Tami can tell you what happened to that man," Kim replied snappishly and began depositing the items back into the fanny pack.

Cody snatched away the molly and told Kim to take the rest to his mother. She didn't object and just nodded her head and then began to take her leave.

"Kim?" Cody called out after her, as she was headed for the door.

Kim glanced back at him.

"Tell Mama I said I love her and that I'll see her soon," he said.

Cody didn't know what he really wanted to say but felt he had to say something.

"I'll tell her, Cody. I promise."

She left the kitchen, leaving Cody to his own addled thoughts.

Who was Rodney Wells? he wondered.

For some reason, Cody began to worry because although he didn't know who the man was, the disturbance he saw in Kim's eyes at the mention of him made him suspicious. Did his mother kill Rodney Wells? That was all Cody wanted to know or else it was going to worry him to death.

***

When the call came, Shawn was in the back room relaxing and waiting to hear from BJ. The ring of the phone next to his head on the bed startled him from his reverie. He had been informed by a reliable source that the people they'd killed were Chuck Murphy's people. His niece was Naomi, and that was more than enough to be concerned over.

"What's up, brah?" Shawn replied, sitting up in bed to take the call.

"Change of plans, my brotha. Some other shit just came up, and we don't need that puppy anymore."

"What, nigga?!" Shawn shot up to his feet. "You know what the fuck me and my people had to go through to snatch that lil boy?"

"Tone down, brah," BJ warned him. "No talk like that over the phone, brah. You know better."

"Fuck that shit, BJ!"

"Shawn…"

Shawn was now pacing the bedroom floor, fury brewing inside of him now. It was one thing having just murdered the niece of a known crime boss but to then have to release the kid too; that was that bullshit.

Sasha appeared in the doorway and looked in on her man, seeing the rage igniting inside of him.

"Let the puppy go, brah. I'll explain everythang to you when I get the chance."

"I don't think you understand the position you're puttin' me in, BJ," said Shawn. "That muthafucker is the least of my worries, brah. We fucked up, BJ."

There was a brief pause.

"Fucked up how? What are you talkin' about, brah?"

"Don't worry about it."

"No. I need to know what happened."

"The phone, remember? I got it, brah," Shawn told him while meeting Sasha's gaze. "You owe me, nigga. I mean, you owe me big time for this shit."

BJ stressed that he was worrying him now and wanted to know what was on Shawn's mind. He reassured him that he had everything under control and that he would do as he was told. Too much had happened in the last hour and a half since taking a child. Chuck Murphy was furious, and his people were out there searching for answers. The killing of his niece was all the fuel he needed to set the streets on fire to smoke out the perpetrators.

After hanging up with his brother, Shawn shared his distress with his woman. No sooner than the words left his mouth did Sasha retreat from the room and hurry up the hallway. He went after her to see what was going on with her rush to get away from him. In the living room, little Shyleek was sitting before the big TV, surrounded by junk food and Juicy Juice containers. Sasha had lain on the floor in front of him while they munched on Oreo cookies and watched cartoons. The scene reminded Shawn of what he had went through with Sasha several months ago when BJ brought his nephew up for a visit. Sasha was all over the boy, purring and coddling him nonstop. She dated Shawn's nephew, and it almost became a problem.

The situation was that Sasha couldn't bear children; she'd been robbed of that chance by two bullets to the stomach. Six times her and Shawn had tried, and she miscarried every time. One almost killed her, and Shawn damn near lost his mind. He knew bringing the boy there to Sasha would pose a very serious problem. Shawn knew this situation was not going to end well between them. Shyleek being there had created tension already.

"Sash." Shawn spoke up when she reached up to tickle the child's chin, and Shyleek giggled.

She looked up at Shawn with a piercing gaze.

"We gotta pack him up to go, baby. It's time," he replied.

"Why can't we keep him, Shawn?" she asked.

Oh, shit, thought Shawn. "You know that's not possible, Sash. It's too dangerous. We've been through this already, baby. It's not happening," he said firmly.

"Fuck you, Shawn," she spat.

He gripped the back of her neck and squeezed. One thing Shawn didn't do was play with her ass. Sasha should know better than to test his patience. He would beat her ass if she got his timing wrong.

"Stop, Shawn! You hurtin' me!" she cried out and tried to wiggle herself free, but his hold was firm.

That was when Shyleek started crying and began slapping the top of Shawn's hand repeatedly. This was his way of trying to protect Sasha from the bad man. Seeing this only made Sasha get extra rowdy. Right then, K-Gutter re-entered the room to see what the commotion was about, but when he saw what was happening, his brotherly instinct kicked in.

"Get the fuck off my sista, dawg!" snapped K-Gutter, shoving Shawn roughly and stepping between them.

It was then that the gun came out, and K-Gutter drew his weapon next. Although K-Gutter considered Shawn something like a big brother and his mentor, his gangsta was not to be denied, and blood was thicker than water.

"You really wanna do this shit, Gutter?" said Shawn, his Glock aimed at K-Gutter's face.

He sneered at Shawn. "You know what I'm bout, brah."

"All I want is the boy."

"You can't have him," said Sasha. "No, Shawn."

She was rocking the child in her arms, trying to calm him. Shy was terrified, and it showed.

"You know this ain't the right move, Gutter."

"It never was to begin wit'," said K-Gutter icily. "Your choice."

Shawn shot K-Gutter dead in the face and turned to Sasha. She turned from him and ran down the hall.

"This bitch gon' make me kill her," he said and went after her.

Having ran into her bedroom and locked the door behind her, Sasha was stunned when Shawn suddenly kicked the door in. He walked right up to his woman and pressed the Glock directly against her forehead.

"Is this how you want it too, baby?"

"Don't take him away from me, Shawn. This is our child. Can't you see that? Can't you fuckin' see that?!" she yelled at him in an outrage.

"Is you gonna give hum up?" he asked.

Sasha hesitated. "I can't," she said softly. "No."

Boom!

Chapter 7

Teddy was sitting in the living room, nursing a glass of cognac that Chastidy had given him. First, she had tended to his wounds, cleaning them and sanitizing them with the proper ointments. Then, she summoned him back to the living room where she poured him a glass of Hennessy. Now, for the last ten minutes, Chastidy had been somewhere in the back doing God knows what

Teddy was still furious with Cody and the others. He felt betrayed and totally disrespected. Bizkit was dead, and that loss was weighing on him hard. He wanted to make Cody bleed for that, and if anybody felt some type of way about it, he would make them bleed as well. The shit had him twisted. He was crossed.

When Chastidy returned, she had in her possession a folder and what appeared to be a manila mailing envelope. She carried herself over to the sofa he was sitting on and dropped down next to him. Out of his peripheral, Teddy gazed down at Chastidy's smooth pecan brown thighs and the trail of paw print tattoos going down her right leg. Chastidy was a bad bitch, sexy as hell, a diva in the flesh, and the ocean breeze body scent that perfumed her was intoxicating. Beyond his own control, Teddy's dick began to stir in his pants. He looked away from her to stare down into his glass.

"What's all that?" he asked.

"This," Chastidy lifted the folder and handed it over to him. "This is your assignment if you're willin' to accept it, Teddy" she said.

"Is this what you was referring to?"

She nodded. "Yeah."

Opening the folder, the first thing Teddy saw was a copy of a photo of a white man. Beneath the photo was the man's statistics and everything about him. Teddy had never seen the man a day in his life.

"Who is he?"

"Read and find out."

"Why won't you just tell me?"

All she did was tap the folder he was holding. There was no need for further explanation because she wasn't giving it. Teddy shifted in his seat, set his glass aside, and began reading the information in front of him.

"His name is Omar Andrade, the son of a reputed arms dealer for the underworld. Unfortunately for Omar, he is now wanted by some very serious people who's willing to pay a quarter million dollars for his assassination."

"Why?" asked Teddy. "What did he do?"

"Read."

And read Teddy did. It turned out Omar had a dire situation with a rival dealer. Somehow, he convinced his rival – a Stuart Downs from Panama City – to meet with him at a secluded location to discuss business that Omar claimed would encourage their differences to be set aside and work as a team. Stu and Omar met as agreed, a mutual agreement was reached, and then when it was finally time to depart, that was when the FBI and the ATF taskforce units swarmed in and wreaked havoc. They rounded up everybody but released Omar several hours later.

"So, he set the other guy up?" Teddy said.

"Sure did," she nodded.

"Then, it's this Stuart guy that's paying to have Omar knocked off?"

"Stu is already dead, Teddy. He was killed months after being locked up. Apparently, a few guys he crossed along the way caught up wit' him in the joint and made him see the error of his ways." Chastidy took up his glass for a taste.

"Then who's paying all this money?" he asked.

"He is called Shadow. No other name is needed if you're really part of that underworld society. When speakin' that name, you better know what you're talkin' about. Anyway, it's him and another guy that goes by the name of Cujo. They're the ones who's fundin' the hit, and due to his respect and solid reputation, Bizkit was given the task. Half of the payment has already been paid upfront. Upon completion of the mission, the second half will be paid."

"If they got that much faith in cuz to do it, why not pay him everything upfront?"

"It's what Bizkit wanted, Teddy."

"But why?"

"I guess you'll have to ask him that in the afterlife," she replied.

Teddy didn't speak for a long moment, as he stared down into his lap in deep thought. He wondered why Shadow and Cujo chose a regular street nigga for the job instead of a professional hired assassin. Did they think Bizkit was expendable? A joke? Because given what Teddy had read so far and what Chastidy had shared with him, killing Omar Andrade would be no easy feat. The man was well protected by the law and his own personal security. How would killing him be easier done than said?

"You got everything you need there to answer whateva other questions you might have."

"Everythang like what?"

Chastidy said, "Bizkit's plans and the strategy he was using to carry out the hit. I'm sure if you study and analyze them, you'll find a way to accomplish the task." She tapped him on the leg and rose up to her feet. "Get it done," she replied, then she walked out the room.

***

Daisy was astride the toilet in the bathroom of her condominium apartment. She and BJ had arrived there right after their visit to the hospital. Daisy wanted to grab a few things, then one thing led to another and BJ had her bent over the bedside driving straight dick into her soul. In all the years they'd known one another, this would be the tenth time they had sex. Their friendship was important, but there was a lot of stress that needed to be released. BJ handled his business like the gangsta he was. No complaints from Daisy.

While astride the toilet, Daisy was startled by the door opening, and BJ flurried into the room. Looking up at BJ, in alarm at the disturbed expression on his face, Daisy wiped, flushed, and rose up immediately.

"She killed herself," said BJ.

"Who?"

"Von," he said.

BJ told her about the phone call that he just received from his boy, Bullet. This was one of the GD gangstas he knew prior to their meeting earlier. Bullet used to come to Havana all the time to visit his uncle, Kake, who lived out in Hinson Heights. When Bullet told him what he witnessed, BJ didn't want to believe it, but then he phoned Rikah on a three-way call, and she confirmed the whole thing.

"Goddamn," muttered Daisy, leaning against the bathroom counter and looking sullen.

To hear Von had committed suicide really threw Daisy. She knew Von was crazy, but to kill yourself was some insane shit.

"Yeah," BJ replied with a sigh. "I never expected her to take herself out like that."

"She did it for her son."

"But she wouldn't do it for her own mama and her girl."

"Wouldn't you die for Bahlil?" Daisy didn't wait for an answer and opened the door to leave.

Despite what her and Von went through, her death was truly affective. Von had really been like a sister to her. They were like two peas in a pod.

BJ went after her and found Daisy standing at the large kitchen counter with a bottle of Grey Goose in her hand. She had this far-away look in her eyes, as BJ eased over to stand beside her and put his hand at the small of her back.

"Dee," he said. "I know you…"

"So, what's the deal with Shyleek?" she asked.

"Shyleek?" he regarded her, puzzled.

"Her son, BJ. Did you call your people to have him let go?"

Daisy put the mouth of the bottle to her lips and took a swig. BJ retrieved his cell phone to call Shawn. Meanwhile, Daisy turned the bottle up again. She was hurting a little over Von's death and needed something to chase it away.

When Shawn finally answered the phone, it wasn't what BJ expected to hear. He told his brother about what he had to do and why.

"Oh, no, Shawn," groaned BJ.

"What?" Daisy froze at the tone of his voice. "What happened, BJ?" she asked.

"So, where is the puppy right now?" BJ ran his hand over his head in a distressed manner.

"I got him right here wit' me, brah. I'm about to drop him off somewhere where somebody can…" Shawn paused for a brief second then cursed in frustration.

"What's wrong, my nigga?"

"Will you please tell me what the fuck is going on, nigga? What is going on? Where is Shyleek?"

For some strange reason, Daisy felt responsible for whatever happened to the child, and that shit was messing with her mental. She felt guilty. If it was not for her, then maybe Von wouldn't be dead right now nor would the little boy be in danger.

"Hold on for a second, Dee," BJ said to her.

"Hold on? Nigga…" Daisy stepped over and snatched the phone from his hand and fumbled with it in her possession, and it fell onto the kitchen floor.

"Dee!"

"I don't wanna hear that bullshit." Daisy squatted down on her hunches to grab the phone.

BJ saw the screen was badly cracked in a spider web fashion, but that didn't affect Daisy, as she brought the phone up to her ear after seeing the connection was still there.

"Hey, Shawn, this is Daisy. What is going on?"

"There's a fifty-thousand-dollar ticket for whoever got information on what went down at the spot," he said.

That made Daisy's eyes turn into slits.

"I just got the text message just now from my partna, Sevin."

"Tell me what the deal is, Shawn."

He told her. "Now, Chuck done put up fifty thousand bands to get intel on who was involved," he explained.

"And who is Chuck? Why is he pressin'?"

"Chuck Murphy's the one who sent that other squad to the spot before we intercepted the ball. Come to find out, his niece was one of the marks."

Shawn continued as he went on to share who Chuck really was and why they all had reason to worry about him. At the same time, BJ told her what he knew where Chuck Murphy was concerned. Then, there was somebody at the door. There was the sound of them buzzing in from the call button outside.

"Where is he, Shawn?" asked Daisy.

"I got'im here wit' me in the car," he answered.

"Where are you takin' him though?"

"Somewhere."

"Somewhere like where, Shawn?" Daisy exited the kitchen for the front door and peered into the video screen mounted on the wall next to the security code pad system.

This system showed whoever came to visit a resident and showed them whenever they would page through. To Daisy's surprise, it was Marlon ringing her, the only other nigga that could say he fucked her on the regular. This was the man her mother liked; he was charming and gangsta at the same time. He and Daisy were somewhat like a couple but not really committed to one another; however, the respect they had for each other was real. Daisy glanced back over her shoulder at BJ.

"I figured he'd show up sooner or later," shrugged BJ, his gaze hard and his chest heaving with adrenaline pumping through him.

She buzzed Marlon up. Daisy wasn't worried about Marlon catching feelings about BJ being there; he was not that type of nigga. The nigga was a player, but his dealings with Daisy were solely righteous. After handing BJ his damaged phone, Daisy opened the front door to wait on Marlon to come up. Across the hall, the neighbor's door opened, and outstepped Terrell Adams, the former hustler turned show promoter.

"What's happenin'?" He nodded in her direction.

"Just maintaining as usual, Terrell."

"Aight then," Terrell replied and swaggered down the carpeted hallway, headed toward the exit.

He never took the elevator down from the fourth floor. He said he didn't trust the mechanism of elevators and tried to avoid them. Daisy knew more about Terrell than he could possibly know about her. He was originally from central Florida and had followed his little sister, Niyahla, up to Tallahassee to watch over her while she attended Florida State University. Niyahla had long graduated over two years ago and returned back down to Orlando, while he remained there. Terrell had obviously found a place where he believed he belonged and had grown a love for the state's capitol. Plus, he was another one of Von's investors. Terrell couldn't resist her charms as well as so many others. The bitch was raw and uncut. Von was charismatic.

Suddenly, the elevator opened at the end of the hallway, and instead of Marlon stepping from it, it was none other than the king of the streets himself: Isaiah. This was Von's man, her significant other, and the only nigga who had ever locked her cold heart down. Daisy figured it wouldn't be long before he showed his face.

Along with Isaiah, four of his shooters followed, and Daisy instantly became guarded by her willingness to survive the storm that was heading her way. A thump in her heart reacted when Daisy saw Marlon lying in a heap on the elevator's floor. She didn't have to inspect him closer to know that Marlon was dead. That shit made her mad.

"Oh, yeah," said Isaiah, as he approached like the prowling, murderous animal that he was. "I knew this time would come one day, Daisy."

Without a response, Daisy ducked back out of sight into her apartment. When BJ looked up and saw her securing the door with its three-lock system, he already knew there was danger amiss and drew his weapon.

"We got a problem," said Daisy.

BJ said, "I see that."

That was when he upped his pistol and pressed it against her temple.

Chapter 8

"I knew Rodney Wells," said Menace, receiving the glass of orange juice Avery handed him.

Come to find out, Menace knew Stefani as well, knew her a whole lot because her mother and him were second cousins on his father's side. Cody was sitting next to his brother, smoking a blunt that was making him so high he didn't even want it anymore. So, he offered it to Stefani who, in turn, smoked her share and passed it to her friends.

"What was wit' him and Mama?" asked Cody.

He knew he was wrong by bringing up the subject when there was a big possibility that his mother could be implicated in something that she'd skated by for this long. Almost twenty years long. Although Menace was hurting like hell, he still managed to remain calm and humbled in spite of his misery. The nigga was tough as polar bear nails.

"Him and your mama used to have the streets in the chokehold back then," said Menace.

"Mama was in the streets?" he asked.

"C'mon, Young C," Menace gave him a hard look. "Look at your mama and how she gets down. She was raised up in the streets. The streets made her who she is today."

All Cody did was nod his head.

"But her way of being in the streets was by robbin' jewelry stores all across the state and even in Georgia."

"Robbin' jewelry stores?" asked Avery, and he cut a glance over at his brother in astonishment.

Menace continued. "Her and Rodney came up that way. Until Rodney got locked up and had to do some time. Your mama kept robbin' them jewelry stores to get up the money Rodney needed to buy himself a good lawyer to get him out of prison."

"Did she get the lawyer?" asked Cody.

"Yep," said Menace. "The best lawyer in the game."

What Cody really wanted to know was how Rodney died and was his mother the killer. He just couldn't shake that concept, his mother being a killer and all. He doubted if Menace would want to revive that subject out of respect for Tami.

"And how much did he do?"

"Five years," said Menace. "He did it to save your mama because that's who them crackaz was after."

That brought Cody upright in his seat.

"Yeah. He saved Tami from doing time and owned up to everythang. Then, when he got out him and Tami decided to make this one last big run that woulda set them straight for a very long time. A lot of people died that day and even Rodney. They pulled the lick off and had got away scot-free. Then, the next morning, they found Rodney in his crib dead as a doorknob. He was stabbed in the heart twice, and his throat was cut from ear to ear. Word on the street was Tami had killed him, but nobody could prove that though. It was just one of them thangs that no one would ever know," Menace said before forcing himself to drink what was left of the glass of orange juice.

Then, he beckoned Stefani up to help him to his feet. After Menace made it to his feet, he asked Stefani to walk him back over next door. She gave Cody a weary glance, not really wanting to leave his sight, but she didn't have the heart to deny Menace anything, so she escorted him back over to Alisha's house. Making her way across the room to follow, Mya took up the rear while Pumpkin remained seated on the couch.

"You not gon' go wit' them?" Avery asked.

"No."

"Why not?"

Pumpkin was the audacious one out of the three; she was bold and sassy. It was she who kept them linked and secured in their faith that they would always stick together. Pumpkin was the fighter, the black sheep, but she was also the sick little kitten in the pack. Pumpkin was epileptic. She had seizures.

"I got some questions of my own," Pumpkin replied, her gaze sharp as barbed wire.

"Questions for who? Me?" said Avery.

"Both of y'all," she said.

The two brothers looked at one another. Cody gave him the look like he wasn't surprised by this. It was so like Pumpkin to want her share of attention.

After scooting her ass up to the edge of her seat, Pumpkin stated, "What're you gonna do now? We know you, Cody, that you killed Stefani's brotha. What's done is done. But what're you gonna do about my girl?" She was looking directly at Cody.

"What do you mean what I'm gon' do about her?" Cody replied.

"Exactly what I mean, nigga," said Pumpkin. "Are you gonna step up now? Because her brotha was her protector, her financial stability. And I know you love her too, Cody," she said, and Cody shifted uneasily in the seat. "You can't lie to me and say that you don't love Stefani. Am I right, Av?"

Avery glanced over at his brother knowingly. "Yep. I already told him that," he said.

"You ain't tell me shit, brah."

Pumpkin said, "Anyway, you will step up now, Cody. And I'm not asking you. I'm not. But what's this thang I'm hearing about Von and y'all beefin'?"

"You know Von?" Avery asked.

She nodded. "Yeah. She saved my life one day when I was sneakin' around wit' this old nigga. But I'm not gonna get into all that..." Her words was cut short when the phone on the table between them started ringing.

Cody reached for it, seeing that it was Menace's cell phone. It was Twan calling, and Cody answered it immediately.

"What's going on, Twan?"

"Oh, shit. Young C, what it do, little gangsta? Where my nigga at?" asked Twan.

Cody shared with him what transpired since the last time they saw each other, about Teddy and the whole situation then about what was told to him by Menace regarding his mother, Tami.

"That's a whole 'nother situation right there, Young C. Talk to your mama yourself and see what she says. And about Teddy, he'll come around. He's just stressing now, Cody."

"He tried to kill me, Twan!" Cody expressed.

"Well," Twan sighed deeply, "then it's either kill or be killed, little brah. I hate to say it, but that's just the way it is, my nigga."

"Would you kill Rod or Menace? Your brothas?"

Twan didn't answer for a long time.

"Yeah," he said. "If it ever came down to it," he paused, "I will."

***

When the trunk of the car opened, Pooh stared up into the cold, hard eyes of Ray Williams. She read murder in his dark gaze. Her heart thumped in her chest, making it hard for her to breathe. Then, he drew back and punched Pooh square in the mouth. Then, he grabbed her by the hair and snatched her from the trunk. Pooh screamed and fought Ray all the way until he slammed her face down into the floor. The sickening crunch of her teeth and her broken nose reverberated off the walls of the room.

"Quit all that damn crying, woman," said Ray.

Stepping around the back of the car, Qay had an expression that spoke monster residing in him. It was as if he was feigning for more bloodshed. Pooh tried to pick herself up from the floor of the garage. Her efforts shattered from the vicious kick to her already injured face by Qay.

"My wife is dead because of your niece," said Ray with a grim expression on his face. "And now you're gonna bring her to me, Pooh. Or else you can die right along wit' the rest of dem fools."

"Y-You gonna k-k-kill me anyway," cried Pooh through the terrifying pain she was experiencing. Her face was pouring out so much blood that it was crazy Pooh was still conscious and hadn't passed out.

"So, you're not gonna give her to me?" asked Ray.

Pooh didn't even acknowledge him. That was when Qay placed the gun against the top of Pooh's head and caressed the trigger.

"Not yet," Ray told him.

Then, he hauled the woman up and shoved her toward the inner side entrance inside the house. To Qay's surprise, the door opened just as Ray lifted his hand for the handle, but it was the person who stood on the other side of that door that made him pause. It was Envy Da Queen, one of the most respected and ambitious divas in the game. Envy was an enemy of many but a breath of fresh air and undeniable beauty and brains to those whose preferences entertained the likes of a transgender individual. Qay looked at Envy, and his trigger finger itched to send one round through their forehead.

"Don't you shoot my son, Qay," said Ray, as he began to shove Pooh forward.

"Son?" Qay gasped. "The fuck…"

Envy frowned and put one hand up in objection.

"How many times I don' told you about referring to me as no-good muthafuckin male counterfeits?!"

"You are a male, boy!"

"Nigga, I'm a lady!" Envy hissed. "Get it t'gether!"

"Move the hell outta my way!" Ray forced Envy backwards to give him space to get Pooh through the door inside the big house.

After they entered, Qay remained standing right where he was, staring at Envy like a snake would eye a rodent. He looked so unsure of what to do. He felt very awkward. For a brief moment, Envy stood there, staring back at Qay with a turned-up nose.

"You coming inside the house or what? Chile, a bitch ain't gon' bite your ass! Plus, you my little sista's man, so I can't bite you even if I wanted to..."

That was when Qay snapped. Before he knew it, he had his hand wrapped around Envy's throat and his gun pushed into her right cheek.

"I should kill you for talkin' to me like that," he growled.

"You can't kill me, boy!" Envy managed to say to him through a strangled voice.

"I'll blow your fuckin' face off."

"Do it then," challenged Envy.

"You think I'm playin' wit' you, bitch?"

Envy sneered.

Qay then redrew himself from Envy, and that was when he shot Envy in the foot. Then, he walked away as if he hadn't done anything. He found Ray in a back room where Pooh was laid out unconscious on the bare bed springs. He had begun bounding both of her hands behind her back when Qay came into the room.

"I knew you wouldn't be able to resist the urge to do something crazy like shootin' my damn son!"

"Does Rayneshia know about this?"

"No."

"Why?"

Ray pretended he didn't ask that stupid question and continued doing what he was doing.

"Because you're ashamed of him," said Qay, already knowing the real reason behind hiding Envy's existence. "How many more children you got out there, Ray?"

"That's all."

"That's all, Ray?" Qay wasn't convinced.

He nodded. "And you're right," Ray paused. "I am ashamed. Been that way since the boy was about nine years old. Funny actin' and shit. Fortunately, he still managed to earn a college degree and now owns a list of businesses. He's very successful. I can tell you that much. But he isn't righteous nor innocent either. He's dangerous, Qay. What I mean by dangerous is this muthafucker is in bed wit' some of the most influential and devious niggaz I've ever seen or heard of. My son is a self-made millionaire, Qay, and all because of the games he plays. One of the games being the downfall of Cojac Montgomery years ago.

"Who the fuck is he?"

"You don't know who Cojac Montgomery is?"

"I mean should I?"

"Maybe you know him by his street handle," said Ray, as Envy cursed and raved continuously, raising all kinds of hell after being shot in the foot. "You might know him by Jack Boy."

It only took a second for the name to register to Qay, and when it did, it stole all the breath out of him.

"No," he muttered. "Not Jack Boy!"

"Tricked right outta his position," said Ray.

Qay shook his head. Not in a million years would he have imagined that happened. That Jack Boy, the son of a crime boss and drug lord who ended up being his dead father's successor, allowed someone like Envy to take him down. But then again, nothing surprised Qay anymore. Jack Boy had not only been powerful but sloppy as well. Apparently, Envy played on his weakness to bring the true him into the light which hindered him into progressing further.

"But I had to kill him in the end," said Ray. "Before he killed my son."

"Jack Boy came back for him?"

Ray nodded. "Good thang I was already watchin' him," he said.

Right then, the detective's phone rang, and he ignored it for a moment, but something told him that he should take the call or he'd regret it. When he reached in his pocket for the phone, he saw that it was Rayneisha calling him. So far, he'd sent her to voicemail five times already and couldn't avoid this one.

"What?" Ray was still bitter with his daughter, another issue he had to deal with.

"You did it, Daddy."

"Did what?"

"Von," she said. "It's all over the internet, Daddy. They found her head in the middle of Tennessee Street."

"Her head?"

"Her head, Daddy. Decapitated. No longer attached to her fuckin' body! Dead," said Rayneisha.

When Ray heard this, he couldn't believe his luck. He knew it had to be true or else Rayneisha wouldn't have wasted time calling him.

"She's dead," whispered Ray. "She's dead."

From somewhere up front, Envy hollered like a wounded animal, but little did Qay know the hell he had created for himself by shooting Envy in the foot.

Chapter 9

Daisy forced herself to turn her head fully around to look at BJ. She couldn't believe this nigga was actually holding a gun against her head, but there was something in BJ's eyes that sent a cold shiver running up her spine. There was coldness there, no emotion, no mercy for what he was doing. Daisy automatically knew there was no talking her way out of this.

"How much money did he pay you, BJ?"

BJ shook his head. "It ain't about no money, Dee. They got my old man and my two kids. I was left wit' no other choice," he said.

Hearing this, Daisy knew without a doubt BJ would see to the mission getting done. Now, she understood the coldness in his eyes. BJ had to force himself to be coldhearted toward her so as not to allow his love for her to disrupt his mission. The nigga was allowed in, and she was not gonna go down that easily. Right then, BJ quickly spun around behind her as though aware of her current thoughts. The gun was now pressed against the back of her head, and BJ bent one of her arms behind her and forced Daisy forward to go unlock the front door.

"Please don't make me kill you, Daisy."

"You won't," Daisy said. "Because then Isaiah would have you killed afterwards."

"Naw. I don't think so. Isaiah's been suggesting for years now that I join the team. I'll use that to my favor and the fact that he got my family to earn his faith that I'll do anything in the world to get them back. I know how to work this situation to my benefit. Of all people, you know how persuasive I am when I want what I want. Now open that fuckin' door before I hurt you," he said.

BJ twisted her left wrist and bent it upwards behind her like the cops had done to him so many times before. Daisy grunted at the pain and growled, but she still moved to unlock the door.

"Just make sure you find me in Hell later when you get there, nigga, because you're not only about to have me killed but your unborn child too," Daisy replied when she disengaged the final lock system.

"What you say?" BJ froze instantly, but the door was already being forced opened.

The first two gunmen entered through the door and went in for the attack on Daisy. The next two entered; one of them drew down on BJ with his mini assault rifle, forcing him backwards. The first two dragged Daisy back farther into the apartment, away from the front door and the possible attempt to escape somehow.

"She's pregnant," said BJ in what sounded like panic.

"So what, nigga?!" Isaiah spat, walking through the door as the thirst of bloodshed showed in his deep brown eyes. Isaiah had a long scar going down the side of his face from a buck-fifty incident back in prison when he had to do some state time. It was there where he caught his first body, then another one, and from there, it gave him a respectable reputation.

"Lemme guess. She's pregnant by you?"

"Yeah," said BJ.

"Then that's just too bad, BJ," Isaiah said before turning his gaze on Daisy's two goons. "Beat that bitch to death," he ordered them.

BJ swallowed nervously. When the beat down began, he flinched, as if he was about to intervene, but the gun pointed at his face stopped him. *Is it true? Is Daisy pregnant for real?*

BJ wondered, as he watched Mega Joe and Keyon throttle Daisy with their fists, feet, pistols, and even a lamp appliance. Was there a child really growing inside of her? Daisy was far from a pushover and was fighting back and fighting hard, no matter the odds that were stacked against her. Then, suddenly, there was a pounding at the front door that alerted them.

"Hold up. Keep her quiet," ordered Isaiah.

Then, he and Pimp moved toward the front door. That was when things got drastic from that point.

"I hope this nigga, Tim, ain't fuck up out there," said Pimp, referring to the fifth goon that was left back to keep the elevator clear of more potential problems they may have.

Just when Pimp reached to open the door, it was forced inward while slamming into him so hard that it jammed two of his fingers and knocked him clean off balance. Terrell entered the room with two guns drawn and shot Pimp dead center of his face. Then, he rushed Isaiah hard before he could react fast enough. He put one of the Glocks to his head and snaked his other arm around his throat as he stepped behind him – all in one fluid motion. He told Isaiah if he breathed wrong, he would kill him dead.

"Now take me to the others," said Terrell.

Inside the great room, Daisy's two assailants were both shot down where they stood. The last thing they expected to see was the prince of the streets himself in the clutches of the enemy. Isaiah couldn't even prevent the inevitable, even if he tried.

"No!" BJ replied. "Don't kill him," he cried. "He knows where my family is!"

"What?" Terrell glared across the room at him.

BJ explained to him what was going on up until the point where Daisy stepped up beside him and blew his brains out the side of his head.

"As you was saying, Isaiah?" Daisy turned her gaze on the big dawg in the room.

Isaiah couldn't even look her in the eyes. He knew he was doomed. A minute ago, he had all the power, and now, the tables had turned.

"Didn't you say earlier that you knew this time would come, nigga?" Daisy had walked right up to Isaiah, her face bloody and swollen, her tired eyes piercing with pure malice in them.

"You can kill me, but you won't get away wit' it though. I got about twenty more killaz waitin' outside the building right now," said Isaiah.

"You mean Tim, Kato, Worm, and the others?" Terrell replied, just behind Isaiah's right ear.

At the mention of his men's names, Isaiah stiffened.

"My people is seeing that they're taken care of."

"You mean your Fed people?"

Terrell nodded. "That's exactly who I mean, Isaiah. Yes. The Feds. Oh. You said it as if it would be a surprise to Daisy? Nah. And since we're speaking of surprises, Isaiah…" he said.

Right then, the team of FBI field agents entered the apartment, and Daisy hurriedly backed herself into a corner. She clutched her murder weapon as she watched Isaiah get cuffed and roughed up by the FBI officials. Then, Terrell reassured one of the others that Daisy was attacked by the dead men, and they had to shoot it out.

"You lied to your people to save me. Why?" Daisy said to Terrell sometime later when they were left alone in the spacious hallway outside of their apartment doors.

"Maybe because I like you, Daisy."

"You like me? Right." Daisy folded her arms across her chest as she looked at him skeptically.

"You have pretty eyes."

"No."

He shrugged. "Okay. Von told me that no matter what the circumstances are, I am to protect you first, and I promised her that I would."

Daisy stared into his eyes. "And that's all she said, Terrell?" she asked.

"No."

"Then what else she said?"

Terrell said, "That you're the big sista she never had and would give her life up for yours if it ever came down to it."

With those words, all Daisy could do was shake her head and walk away. She still couldn't believe Von was dead, her little sister. The same bitch she would have given her life for if it ever came down to it.

***

Teddy pulled the shiny red Chevy Caprice Classic up to the stop sign and stopped. He took a deep breath and then gazed over to his right. Setting in the passenger seat was a duffel bag filled with money, guns, and all the essentials from Bizkit's home safe that he planned to use to his benefit. Thanks to Chastidy, he now had the motivation and the power to move a mountain. He would honor Bizkit's legacy. His brief talk with Shadow minutes ago confirmed everything he needed to make his new journey progressive. Then, there was Cujo, the elder business mogul and leader of his own crime syndicate. Shadow guaranteed Teddy that he would consult with the old man on his behalf, but for the most part, Teddy was to do his part to show and prove his worth.

Teddy pressed forward, as he drove through his old stomping grounds in his cousin's car. So much was going on around him. A whole new order was in store for the streets of Quincy, and he was about to set it in motion. But first, he needed to appoint himself a new right hand man. That was pretty simple enough to decide because there was only one other person outside of his brothers that was worthy, and that was his homeboy, Ritchie.

In passing, people who expected to see Bizkit driving but saw Teddy were filled with surprise, but then they nodded in acknowledgement and saluted him as he drove on. People knew by now that Bizkit was dead, and now seeing Teddy lurking through the streets in his car... That presence alone was enough to make onlookers wonder.

Teddy was not the same young knucklehead everybody knew him as. He used to be called Money Mel's little brotha. Now, he was adopting the name Beast Mode Teddy. The scarred face and his newfound malicious attitude outlined the description of a beast. He found Richie where he knew he would, which was in the alleyway between his house and the old bando next to it. Teddy pulled the car up alongside the mouth of the alley on the street. Richie was in the process of serving two crackheads when he saw the Chevy Caprice pull up.

"Check it out when you're done," said Teddy through the driver side window, beckoning Ritchie over to the car with the wave of the hand.

When Ritchie saw this, he served product to one of the customers and hurried in Teddy's direction. Behind him, the emptyhanded crackhead called out after Ritchie, who kept moving forward. From his position behind the wheel, Teddy watched Richie come to a sudden halt. He looked back over his shoulder at something the crackhead had said to his back. Then, he spun on his heels and marched right back in the direction of the now anxious looking customer.

"Oh, shit," Teddy muttered when he saw Ritchie reach behind him and bring forward the 9mm pistol.

He flipped the pistol barrel into his grasp and bashed the man in the face with it. Then, he flipped the handle back into his palm and shot the crackhead in the ass. Ritchie kicked him in the back when he fell to the ground, hollering. The crackhead who had already been served was long gone after he heard the slick shit that was said to Ritchie's back. After making the crackhead get up and limp away out of the alleyway, Ritchie retracked his journey back toward the Chevy Caprice.

In the back of his mind, Teddy was thinking how smart it was to link up with Ritchie. The young nigga was wild, fearless, intelligent, plus he always had Teddy's best interest at heart. For an eighteen-year-old, Ritchie had gone through some grimy situations, had survived the inevitable, and he was still striving to reach his potential of being a thoroughbred gangsta.

"Get on the other side," said Teddy.

He didn't even have to tell him because Ritchie was already stepping around the other side. In the process, Teddy hefted up the duffel bag and set it on the backseat behind him.

"What it do?" Ritchie squeezed his chubby frame into the passenger seat next to his homeboy.

Teddy gave him some dap, and they sat there for a quiet moment.

"Why did you shoot Hoppo?" asked Teddy.

Ritchie waved him off, but Teddy persisted on knowing.

"You saw what was going down. I saw you and didn't care about serving that nigga. Hoppo owed me 'bout thirty dollars anyway," said Ritchie, his fresh crisp Gucci T-shirt a size too small on his big frame. "The stupid nigga tried to use my pops as reference that I should serve him or regret it."

"But ain't Hoppo your cousin too?"

"So what?"

"You wild as hell, Ritchie, which is one of the reasons why I'm here," said Teddy.

Ritchie fired up a Newport. "What's up?"

He and Teddy could go for twin brothers; both of them were fat and hotheaded, but Teddy was a whole other animal that Ritchie was soon to find out.

"You know me and Cody and Av ain't brothas no more, Ritchie," Teddy replied.

"What happened?"

When Ritchie's father was murdered two years ago, both Avery and Teddy had come over to the house to give him moral support. It was then that Richie turned up and hadn't turned down since. Teddy told him where the beef transferred from.

"And now I'm Bizkit's successor, brah. And I need somebody like you as my right-hand man," he added.

"You already know I'm wit' it, brah." Ritchie extended his meaty left fist, and Teddy bumped it with his own, sealing the promise to stick together.

"But there's something I need you to do first."

"What?"

With that being said, Teddy put the car in gear and drove them in the direction of Key Street. In the process, Teddy told him what he wanted in the way of Ritchie solidifying his position. In turn, Ritchie retrieved the Mac-90 assault rifle from the duffel in the backseat and prepared himself for what he was about to do.

"You serious about this, huh, Teddy?"

Teddy didn't answer.

Minutes later, the Chevy Caprice was easing down the street in the direction of Cody's house. Teddy told him the house wasn't empty, that Cody was inside, and Ritchie needed no further motivation. Ritchie lifted the assault rifle, turned sideways in his seat, and when Cody's house came into his line of sight, he squeezed the trigger. Hail Mary in Pepper Hill once again. It was ugly.

Chapter 10

Tami glanced over at Bebop's bed longingly as her conversation with Kim caused her to go into deep thought. She worried over whatever her son might know about her old lifestyle as a robber and a killer. Her life standing on the side of Rodney Wells was something like you saw in the movies.

Her past life was an urban book of its own, and for some reason, Tami felt like her past sins were coming back to haunt her through her son's situation. Karma was a bitch!

"So, you didn't tell him nothing, Kim?" Tami hoped she didn't tell Cody anything when she didn't know what really happened all those years ago.

"I told him he would have to ask you what he wanted to know about the situation."

"But he knows there's a situation."

Kim nodded. "But he got Menace there wit' him, and it ain't no tellin' what he told him," she said, intentionally throwing all the heat off herself.

The black fanny pack was in her hand, and Tami had one of the packages of Molly in her palm; she had discreetly cuffed it earlier when her desire to pop some Molly was strong. Now, she didn't feel the urge to do so because a stronger want for her son's respect was just as powerful. Tami got up with the fanny pack; she entered the bathroom. No sooner than the door shut closed did the room door open, and Faye and Quick, her nephew, was heard engaging in talk with two other voices that Tami didn't recognize.

In the bathroom, Tami had some serious decision-making to do. Before she allowed her thoughts to take the wrong course, Tami went into action. All the Molly she was in possession of, Tami dumped all the contents of all six packages she had, almost $2,500 worth of product wholesale. Tami was tired of the struggle of fighting her habit to abuse her Molly stash. Now, she no longer had her stash. It was all gone and flushed down the toilet drain. That urge to jump in after the drugs was heavy on her, but Tami knew she had to overcome that. It was time for a fresh start.

Next, Tami removed the leather wallet from the pack and was about to rip it to pieces too, but something made her stop. It was another familiar voice she heard in the room that made her believe some shit was about to go down. Tami opened the bathroom door and stepped out to see Susie sharing the room with the others. This was Wesley's god sister, and she had on her uniform scrubs. Susie was a registered nurse there at Tallahassee Memorial Hospital. When she turned at the sudden presence of Tami, Susie cut her words short and directed her attention solely on her.

"Yeah. I'm here, Tami," said Susie. "I came to see what you're doing."

"Why you checkin' on me, Susie? You ain't been doing it, so why start now?"

Susan Miller was a tall, big boned woman, blacker than black but pretty for a fifty-one year old woman. Tami had to look up at the other woman, as she towered over her by at least six inches.

"It seems Wesley being dead doesn't mean anything to you. Why? Because I've checked wit' damn near all the local funeral homes, and not one of them are in preparation for my brotha's burial. But yet here you are, takin' up unnecessary space up in here worrying over another's woman's child while Wes is laid up rotting on some…"

This time, Kim beat Tami to the punch and popped Susie dead in her mouth. The woman staggered backwards into Quick, who instantly caught her fall before she hit the floor.

"You talk too damn much," said Tami. "I remember tellin' you once your slick ass mouth gon' get you in some mess."

"I never liked the heifer anyhow," said Kim.

Then, from the fanny pack, Tami extracted a thick roll of rubber band bound bills. Tami estimated the cash to being ten thousand and then tossed it at Susie, who let the money bounce off her chest.

"That should get Wes a proper burial for now," said Tami. "Since you got so much to damn say."

"Why I gotta do it fo'?" said Susie through bloody teeth.

"Cause you talk too much," Tami answered.

Susie frowned and gazed down at the money as if she was contemplating picking it up. Right then, the door burst open, and both Twan and Rod came barging in. Rod said something about turning on the news channel on the TV, and Kim reached for the remote control.

"Von," muttered Tami moments later when the close-up photo of Von was plastered on the TV screen.

The title read: *Local Drug Lord Found Beheaded,* and the news reporter was standing near the scene where she said the severed head was found.

"Damn," Twan whispered. "Isaiah is about to snap!"

Behind them, Susie bent forward to pick up the money and made her exit. Kim them went after her to make sure she had good intentions in mind.

"So, that's the young lady that everybody's been going crazy about lately," said Faye. "Now look what her bad decisions don' got her."

"Shut the hell up, Faye. Damn!" Tami shushed her with a hand.

As she listened to what the news reporter had to say about Von's situation, Tami thought about Von's father lying down in the room next door.

"Over a hundred homicides!" Faye gasped when the Leon County sheriff himself appeared on the screen before the reporter, giving what he knew of Von and her crime history.

Apparently, Von had been busy for a very long time to be assumed responsible for over a hundred homicides. Her street affiliation went back to when Hooliganz Crime Gang was running the streets years ago. Von was considered a kingpin, a manipulator, a businesswoman, and a killer.

"But isn't it true that this same killer funded Mayor Bridgette Matthews' election campaign?" asked the news reporter, and from the looks of the sheriff's reaction, he appeared sickened by her bold inquiry.

"I have no knowledge of anything of that nature, ma'am. Sorry, but I have work to do," said Sheriff Tom Bowen, and he made his hasty retreat.

"Mayor Matthews? Wow," Faye replied. "That woman is coming for the mayor, and that right there just might get her what she's lookin' for."

"Or what she ain't lookin' for," added Rod, knowing situations like that could get you killed.

But he too was shocked by the whole matter of Von financing the mayor's campaign, which probably played a major part in her winning her second term.

Tami switched off the TV and had to take a seat before she lost her footing. To hear that Von was dead and beheaded was so surreal.

"So, you knew about this?" asked Tami, looking up at Twan and folding her arms.

Outside the room door were two goons Twan had employed to watch over her and Bebop. One of them, Brico, re-entered the room behind Kim and beelined it straight to where Rod was standing amongst them.

"That's the least of your worries right now, Tami," said Twan, as Rod and Brico spoke in hushed tones.

"So, what should I worry about then?" she asked.

Reluctantly, Twan told her about Cody and Teddy's beef and where she stood in becoming a victim or a savior because, at the end of the day, she was both of their mother, including Felicia and Shequita, both of whom Twan had already spoken to as well. There was no influence like Tami's influence, the one that had many a time brought an end to a lot of catastrophes where the boys were concerned.

Across the room, Bebop groaned in discomfort, as he lay medicated in his bed. Instantly, Tami rushed to his bedside.

"Where the fuck is Ms. Thang anyway?" asked Twan.

There was no answer from Tami, as she dabbed a cloth onto Bebop's damp forehead.

Twan inquired about Bebop's mother – his real mother, who was a severe drug addict and had never had her son's best interest at heart. The boy didn't even know who his father was. The streets raised him with the parents of his brothers, Cody, Teddy, and the twins.

"I need to talk to my son," said Tami.

Twan whipped out his phone and said, "I think that'll be what you both need right now."

***

Avery and Pumpkin had been going back-and-forth while Cody stared at the picture of Von that was being uploaded on all social media sites. Her death was circulating around like a fierce wildfire. They had found her head but not her body yet. There was no telling how the rest of Von's body was going to be discovered.

That was what Avery and Pumpkin were going back-and-forth about, the discovery of Von's body while using references to certain movies where similar scenarios had taken place. Then, Avery got up to go into the kitchen for something to drink.

"I'm telling y'all, Cody." Pumpkin directed her attention on him next. "They're gonna drop her body off piece by piece as a warning to everybody that she wasn't untouchable like everybody thought she was, and whoever feel some type of way about it, they'll get the same shit done to them," she said.

"You watch too many movies," said Cody.

Pumpkin shrugged and said, "Well, she's dead now, and a lot of people out there can finally breathe now."

"She wasn't no goddamn boogeyman!"

"Not according to others."

"You?" he asked.

"Hell no!" Pumpkin replied. "I didn't even know Von," she half-lied.

"Yet you seem to know about her."

"That's because I keep my ears to the streets, Cody. My girlfriend, Monika's sista, Lana, was working for her over in Tallahassee at her nail shop."

Avery came in and said, "What's up wit' this plan Daisy claimed she had…" His words was cut short by the sudden explosion of automatic rounds ringing out from outside.

Bullets penetrated the walls of the house, and to Cody's horror, he watched Avery's body jerk violently, as hot slugs ripped into him.

"Av!" Cody lunged for his brother, but it was already too late because by the time he reached Avery, his body spasmed for a second and then nothing. "Noo! Get up, Av! Get up!" he cried, trying to shake Avery awake, but it was no use.

"Cody, you're bleeding!" said Pumpkin.

The words seemed to not have registered to Cody because he was still kneeling over his dead brother, crying quietly and staring down at Avery in disbelief, and Pumpkin moved forward to offer him some comfort. The instant her hand touched his shoulder, Cody flinched, spun upward at a one hundred eighty degree turn, and wrapped a fist into the front of her shirt. Then out came the gun and was placed right against Pumpkin's head.

"Cody! Baby, stop! Stop!" Stefani screamed from the doorway of the hallway.

She came running through the back door after the shots ceased. When Cody turned to look in her direction, he was caught off guard when Stefani closed in on them and wrapped her loving arms around him. Then, she told him how much she loved him and that it would hurt her if he hurt Pumpkin. She kept right on talking softly to him until Cody released Pumpkin, and Stefani wrapped that arm around her next. Maya appeared in the room next, and Pumpkin ran into her arms.

"Fuck! Fuck! Fuck!" Menace snapped in an outrage when he saw Avery laid out on the floor. "This is so fucked up," he said.

Then, out of nowhere, Menace slumped to the floor, unconscious.

"Oh, no!" Maya cried out.

Looking back to Menace also on the floor made Stefani want to scream. So, she turned back around, buried her face into Cody's chest, and screamed with all her might. Outside, car tires were heard screeching to a stop, as Money Mel's voice was also heard barking out orders, as he neared the front door.

The front door opened, and there stood Money Mel and Po' Boy, and just beyond them, Felicia and Shequita were coming cautiously up the rear. When Money Mel saw Avery, he damn near fell to his knees. Then, he spun back for the doorway and moved forward to block the women's path, specifically Felicia's. He placed his hand on her chest, and she looked up into his distraught face questioningly.

"My baby?" asked Felicia.

He shook his head sadly. What happened next was heartbreaking. Felicia bellowed and fell to her knees. Then, she got right back up and made an attempt to get through the door. Felicia wanted to see her son. Money Mel told her not like this. So, she fought him physically. Shequita didn't intervene because she knew her son could take it, but what Shequita did do was enter the house herself.

"You can't come in here, Mama," said Cody, who suddenly appeared in the foyer, blocking her path.

"I got her, lil brah," Po' Boy replied.

He came up behind Cody and laid a hand upon his shoulder, the very same thing that almost got Pumpkin shot. With a shake of his head, Cody slowly stepped outside and right into the furnace of Felicia's sorrow, and it was painful to watch.

"Ma," said Cody after a brief moment, then he moved forward to take one of her hands into his.

He had to hold on tightly to prevent her from pulling away from him, but by this time, her struggle with Money Mel had tired her out. So, with Cody's contact, he just pulled her easily into his arms.

"My baby!" cried Felicia against him.

This only added more fuel to Cody's rage. He was hardening by the minute, and before long, there wouldn't be any more feeling coming through him. His brother was dead. That was a whole different type of pain. It was murder.

Chapter 11

About nineteen minutes later, Po' Boy entered Alisha's house from the front door. Cody and the others were occupying the living room. Next door, once again, Cody's house was crawling with CSI people. In the last forty-eight hours, so many people had died there. Shequita was beginning to think the house was cursed.

"I need to talk to you, brah." Po' Boy pointed at Money Mel then at Cody next. "You too. Right now," he demanded.

"Whateva you gotta say, Po' Boy, you can say that shit right here," said Stefani, speaking for Felicia, who was resting her head upon her shoulder on the sofa.

"She's right, Po' Boy. We all family here. No secrets. What's up?" Mel said.

Before Po' Boy could answer, there was a knock at the front door. Maya moved to go answer it while everybody else remained where they were.

"It's some old lady out there," said Maya.

"Open the door," Po' Boy told her.

When the door opened, the last person they expected to see was Diana 'DeeDee' Peoples. This was Pepper Hill's grandmother, the grandmother of the whole community, the woman who had been carrying Pepper Hill on her back for over sixty years and counting. At eighty-four years old, DeeDee looked no older than sixty, except for her headful of long, gray hair showering down her back. Overall, she moved with a purpose, and when DeeDee was present, her honor and respect was due or else be prepared to get rebuked for not doing so. So, upon her entrance, those who knew her stood up and greeted her with a hug. This was royalty. DeeDee watched this hood grow from the root, and it was with love for her people that she watered that root until it sprouted to something beautiful throughout the last six decades.

Felicia was the last one who embraced the old lady, burying her face into her bosom like she'd done many times before. Both Pumpkin and Maya stood by, watching the exchange, as they wondered just who this old woman was.

"As of right now," said DeeDee, short but stocky built and as lovely as ever, "that house over yonda is considered condemned. No family should ever live in that house again. So, my child," she swiveled her gaze over at Cody, "you need to see that it gets done right away."

"What you want me to do, DeeDee?" asked Cody.

"Whateva you feel is best, my child."

Cody nodded.

"And secondly," the old lady continued, "whateva this is y'all got going on, it's breakin' my heart. My heart can't take too much as it is. But we've loss too many of our own wit' this mess, and it needs to stop. I'm telling you to put an end to it. Now!"

"That's what we're doing, DeeDee."

"But more people are dying in the process, Melvin. You of all people should know better. I've watched you run these streets since you was knee high. You were destined to lead. Be the leader that you are. Stop followin' the blood trail for your next victim. Stop followin' your heart for a change and lead wit' this." DeeDee tapped the side of her head with two fingers.

For the next ten minutes, they all heard DeeDee out, as she dropped precious jewels of wisdom on them. Then, she ordered the fellas to be dismissed while she sat with the ladies for a while. Po' Boy, Money Mel, and Cody retired to the back of the house where Menace was resting on the couch in the large den area. Menace had lost so much blood, and on top of that, the emotional strain he was enduring was what knocked him unconscious earlier. The nigga was just too stubborn. He was purpose driven; his willpower to stay alive amidst the war was beyond commendable. He just wouldn't allow himself rest.

Menace just needed to sit his ass down somewhere and stay put. Like now. It was as if he was waiting on the moment for them to come in. Soon as they walked into the room, Menace forced himself to sit up.

"We takin' your ass to the hospital, nigga," Cody said to Menace, who just stared at him through glossy eyes. "Don't look at me like that, Menace. You need help, big brah."

"Teddy did it," Po' Boy interjected.

Money Mel looked over at his road dawg. "How do you know Teddy did this?"

"A few people told me they saw him ridin' round in Bizkit's Chevy earlier. The same Chevy that did the drive-by. But he wasn't alone neither," said Po' Boy. "Somehow, he convinced young Ritchie to roll wit' him, and we all know how he put it down. He shot Hoppo in the ass round the corner in the alley. This shit just got even more realer now that lil brah is dead, and Teddy is out there on dumb shit."

"Chastidy," said Money Mel.

"Huh?"

"He had to go to her in order to get the Chevy."

For a minute, Money Mel felt a wave of jealousy wash over him at the thought of Teddy going through all this over their cousin's death. Bizkit was family and all, but Teddy was Money Mel's little brother, the very same little brother he adored like crazy. Money Mel was jealous of the effect Bizkit had on his little brother even in death. Pulling out his phone next, Money Mel put a call through to Chastidy.

"I've been expecting your call," Chastidy answered.

"Did Teddy come to you?" he asked.

"Yes, he did, Mel. Why?"

"What for?"

Chastidy didn't hold anything back from him and told Money Mel what the deal was. It didn't take much for him to see that Teddy was now stepping into his cousin's shoes. That shit was playing on Money Mel's pride, and it was seriously affective.

"Where did he say he was going after he left you, Chaz?" Money Mel called her by her nickname.

She said he didn't say, only that he was gonna stay in touch. Right then, Po' Boy tapped him on the shoulder. When Money Mel looked at him, he saw worry in his eyes.

"What is it, my nigga?"

"Lil brah don' dipped on us," said Po' Boy.

Sweeping the room and not finding Cody present, Money Mel hurried out of the room to go look for him. What he feared was what was already done. Cody was gone. He was going after Teddy alone.

***

Shawn had completed his task. He dropped the boy off in the parking lot of a local supermarket in downtown Jacksonville. He let Shyleek out and told him to go inside the supermarket. After he watched the boy do that, Shawn then got missing. He wanted no other dealings with the boy whatsoever.

Back in traffic, Shawn was putting a call through to his brother when a premonition came over him. The phone rang four times before it was answered.

"Brah? You got me fucked up, BJ. I don' lost everythang fuckin' wit' you and your bullshit."

"Hello, Shawn," another voice replied.

Shawn froze. "Who dis?"

"David Bradwell."

"I don't know no David Bradwell. The fuck you doin' answering my brotha's phone?! Where BJ at?" snapped Shawn, swerving a little as he drove.

"Okay. Lemme be more specific for you. I'm Special Agent in charge David Bradwell wit' the Tallahassee FBI unit. Your brotha, Shawn, is in federal custody right now, and if you're smart..." Shawn hung up on him before he could finish whatever he had to say.

"Fuck!" he cursed. Shawn knew something was wrong; he felt it in his heart.

If the FBI really had his brother in custody, then where would that put him? Would BJ implicate him in the murder and kidnapping of Shyleek?

"This shit is crazy," muttered Shawn.

Now, his paranoia was on high alert. Shawn didn't trust BJ to stay solid against the Feds. He'd known him too long and knew how far BJ could go before he broke. The Feds played hardball, and what they had in store for BJ was not going to be pretty.

The phone sounded off with an incoming call from BJ's baby mama's sister, Rhondra. He snatched the phone up and answered it.

"What's up, Rhondra?"

"You need to get down here, Shawn," she said. "I don't know what's going on, but some niggaz kidnapped your daddy and your two nieces. They beat Ceiara almost to death, and now, BJ is nowhere to be found. You need to get over here asap, Shawn!" said Rhondra.

At hearing BJ's father had been abducted along with his two daughters, Shawn felt very disturbed by the situation. He and BJ shared different fathers but the same mother. However, Shawn felt motivated to do something about it because if the shoe was on the other foot, BJ would as well.

"Okay. I'm on my way, Rhondra."

"You don't sound too concerned to me, Shawn."

"That's because I don't overreact, Rhondra. I'm built differently than most…"

Shawn was peering in his rearview mirror when he spotted the black Chevy Tahoe tailing him. At first, when he saw the SUV, he assumed it was just swerving through traffic like all the other cars, but that was fifteen minutes ago. Shawn had taken multiple routes since then. He was now convinced the black truck two cars behind him was actually following him.

Shawn disconnected with Rhondra and proceeded to keep his place in traffic. Once he let on that he'd spotted the tail, things could turn from bad to worse real fast.

"Don't panic," Shawn told himself.

It was clear whoever was following him didn't want him dead just yet. They had all the opportunity in the world to step on him, which made Shawn believe they wanted something from him and then he'd die.

"Got me fucked up if you think I'm that fuckin' sweet," said Shawn aggressively.

Word was already out that Chuck Murphy had put out a big money bag for information on who was responsible for the murders of his niece and her crew. Shawn already knew the stakes were high, which meant that he needed to tie up serious loose ends, and that loose end was his cousin, Tap. Yeah, Tap was deviously money hungry and would sell Shawn out in a heartbeat to collect that ticket.

Tap was Shawn's reliable resource that had been keeping him informed on things outside of their own personal business. If he thought he could get away with it, Tap would feed him to the wolves. Family was always the first ones to cross you and when you least expected it, which was why Shawn was grabbing a hold of the big .45 caliber he had resting in the passenger seat. That bad boy was already fully loaded with two extra fully loaded magazines.

"Let's rock out then," said Shawn, bringing his car up to a red light behind two other vehicles.

In the process, Shawn donned a black ski mask that he always had on hand just in case of situations like this one. The car slowed to a stop along with traffic, and Shawn put the gear in park. He took a deep breath, cocked back the slide on his gun, opened the door, and got out.

"You wanna fuck wit' me!" Shawn shouted, as he lifted the big .45, aimed, and began sending rounds slamming into the SUV.

As he let loose on the unseen enemy, Shawn closed in on the truck. He was so focused on what was in front of him that he didn't notice the two shooters coming up behind him. The whole time, there was a team of killaz riding in the car in front of him. The SUV succumbed to the .45's wrath, as its occupants screamed and ducked down inside. Slugs were soaring through the windshield and its metal exterior, as Shawn didn't let up on the trigger, but that was until he felt something strike him in the back of the head. It dazed him and sent him lurching forward, but Shawn managed to keep his balance. Then, he turned around to see who his assailant was and couldn't believe his eyes.

"Tap," he replied.

Without mercy, Tap squeezed the trigger on his AK-47, shooting his own cousin to death. Hot slugs ripped through Shawn's chest, as explosions of blood and bone fragments shot off from his body right there in the middle of traffic in Jacksonville, Florida in front of the whole city. Another nigga killed his own flesh and blood for that money bag, just like Shawn knew he would. There was no honor amongst kin, not even a little bit.

Chapter 12

Cody slipped away through the patio door silently. He needed to separate himself from Money Mel and the wicked thoughts he was struggling to keep at bay where Teddy's life was concerned. Teddy had to die. He'd really gone off the deep end and gotten Avery killed, his best friend, his own brother, and he was probably so caught up in his own darkness that he couldn't see the bigger picture. He was so much on go-mode, the demons inside of him commanded him. All Teddy knew now was drill, and that mind frame would get him killed.

Cody wanted his head for that, for Avery. Just now, he was contemplating blowing Money Mel's brains out. It was just that serious now. He forced himself to control that monster in him, but Lord knows he was a split second away from killin' his big brother. Plus, all types of policemen were out front and next door. One shot was all they needed to hear to bum-rush the spot. Then, there was Shequita to think about too. If Cody killed Money Mel, then she would have to die too.

The beast was beating his insides up to free itself from its confines, but all Cody needed to hear was that Ritchie was involved in the equation because if Teddy was driving, then that left Ritchie as the triggerman, which meant Cody should hit him back with someone he loved then take him personally out the game next.

Ritchie lived with his grandmother, Peggie, over on 2nd Street. Cody knew all the paths and back trails that led to where Ritchie lived. Within minutes, he made it to the back alley where Ritchie hung out with his crew, slanging hard and soft. When Cody stepped out from the path into the alleyway, he saw Bonnie perched on a stack of crates, puffing a blunt. He was one of Ritchie's road dawgs, and Cody knew he had to have him too.

"What's up, Bonnie?" he replied.

Startled, Bonnie came off his sitting position and stood up to face Cody.

"Damn, nigga. Don't be sneakin' up on a muthafucka like that. What's up?" said Bonnie, a much older nigga who was originally from the East Quincy area.

He stuck out his fist for some dap, and Cody showed him some love.

"What's going on 'round here?" asked Cody.

"C'mon, Cody. Whatchu lurkin' 'round for? Heard you been puttin' in some work lately. Who you lookin' for, my nigga?" Bonnie wasn't dumb by a long shot.

He knew Cody was up to no good. Cody didn't frequent this part of the hood, and his being there raised questions with Bonnie.

"What makes you think I'm lookin' for anybody?"

"Do I look stupid to you, Cody?"

Cody shrugged. Then, he drew his gun and shot Bonnie once in the face. Then, he stepped over him and put another one in his chest. Next, Cody slid alongside of Ritchie's house and around back where he expected to kick in the back door and find Peggie inside, but there she was, hanging up clothes in the backyard. She'd survived seventy-two years through some of the greatest racism and tragedies in history only to stare down the barrel of Cody's gun, and without blinking, she took her two bullets to the face like the fearless woman she was. She died lying on top of Ritchie's favorite Chicago Bulls basketball jersey she'd just washed.

Cody ducked off, back through the alley into the back path from which he came. A minute later, he came out onto

Stewart Street Road where a gray Ford Mustang blared its horn behind him, approaching his way. Cody turned back to see that it was Rikah behind the wheel. Behind her, two black cars pulled over to the side of the street along with hers. Rikah hung out her side window and told him to get inside. At the same time, Tuk got out from the passenger side of the Mustang and hurried off for one of the two cars waiting behind it and got in. Cody got in the Mustang, and they were off into traffic, heading north toward town.

"Where you coming from, Cody?" she asked.

Rikah had always been good to Cody whenever she was around long enough to see him. He remembered her more than he did Daisy.

"I heard Mel talkin' wit' Twan, so you was there when it happened?" asked Cody.

"When what happened?"

"Von," he said.

Hesitantly, Rikah nodded. "Yeah. It's over where Von is concerned. She's dead and gone. But you, lil cuzzin, I hear you turnt up out here," she said.

Cody didn't reply.

"I know about Avery too, Cody."

He turned his gaze at her. "How?" he asked.

"Does it even matter? What should matter is how you gon' handle it. Because at the end of the day, you'll be gunnin' for your best friend, your brotha – not no other lame ass nigga in the streets."

"I can't let him get away wit' that, Rikah. Teddy has to die. That's the only way to stop him."

"And Melvin?"

"What about him?"

"You really think he's gonna just let you murder his baby brotha and charge it to the game?" Rikah replied. "Hell no!" she added.

That was when Cody told her about his wicked thoughts earlier, thoughts that led him to killin' two others just a minute ago.

"Hmph." Rikah shifted in her seat. "Figured your ass was up to something just now. It was written all over your face, cuzzin."

"My face?"

"That killa scowl. That look. That one that warns of destruction if crossed," she said.

There was a momentary silence before Rikah's phone rang, and she answered it gracefully.

"What's up, babe? Oh, yeah. Good. We need to link up, babe. All types of shit been going down since you been gone." Rikah sighed, as she listened to what was being said on the other end of the phone.

Meanwhile, Cody had his gun out and was checking the clip. There was only two bullets left in the clip. He needed to dispose of this one and get another banger that was fully equipped with ammo and extra magazines. The way things were going, being strapped with that tool was a necessity.

"That was Joshua," said Rikah.

"What's up with him?" Cody asked, slapping the clip back into the gun.

"He had to take that trip to Cuba to personally meet up wit' his connect. He had heard about all the shit that was going on here and came back home."

"He came back for you."

Rikah smirked. "Jay know I can handle my own. I'm no weak bitch who tucks her tail and runs when the pressure is on. I take care of business, cuzzin. I wasn't put in this position for nothin'."

"Von thought the same thing."

"But look where tha shit got her ass."

"Dead."

"Apparently." Rikah described the whole incident in more grave details than she did before. She wanted to remind

Cody how easy it was to become a victim to your own destruction when you felt untouchable.

"And are you untouchable?"

"No."

He nodded.

"I'm human. I'm not immortal. But if it ever came down to puttin' in that work, I do it good. I get it done properly, cuzzin."

To Cody, his cousin sounded too full of herself, self-centered, arrogant, but in all actuality, Rikah was no different from Von. Von was dead, and Rikah could have just as well been her too.

Teddy was his issue now. Whatever he thought he had going on, Cody was planning on stopping that. Teddy was trapped in his own darkness. He needed some lightening up – light from that cannon just before everything went bright before he died – for Avery.

***

Daisy peeped into the room then stepped inside where she came face to face with Chloe standing at Vincent Roberts' bedside. She was crying while holding the man's hand, who was still in a coma, and it wasn't looking promising. Also present was someone Daisy didn't know personally but had seen around town. He was not much younger than Vince himself, well-fit, and serious looking – like a man used to having his way.

Daisy said, "How is he?"

"With all that's happened, I think it's best that he remain in the position he's in. His wife is dead, Von is dead, everybody he ever loved is gone," said Chloe, her misty brown eyes shining with emotion.

"Everybody except for you, Daisy," said the male stranger, rising up to his feet to extend his hand. "I'm Amos Betsey, a very good friend of Vince."

"And I'm supposed to know you?" said Daisy.

"You should," he said.

Daisy shot the man a sharp gaze. "Why do I feel you are more than just a simple man who came to visit your friend?"

"Because I'm not."

"Then who are you really?"

He stroked his salt and pepper beard. "The matter isn't really about who I am but what am I, Daisy."

"A muthafuckin' riddle?" she retorted.

He chuckled. "No," he said. "My name is Shadow."

The instant he said the name, Daisy perked up, and her heart began to race. This was a name she only heard about but never could put a face to it. But what surprised her even more was the fact that she'd seen him on several occasions but didn't know he was the stone-cold killer and crime boss and a man accepted into the secret society of the underworld due to his influence. Shadow indeed led the life of a regular guy during the day, but at night, he was everything that promoted fear in the hearts of many. His name was Shadow for a reason; it came with many tragedies and power.

"And I know all about you, Daisy," he said.

"What you know about me?" Daisy was really intrigued over the fact that she was sharing the room with a man as great as Shadow.

Then, he blew her mind by what came out of his mouth next. The first thing was one of Daisy's earlier kills back in the day when she robbed the pizza delivery man and stabbed him. Then, her mother had kicked her out the house, and she was living on the streets, trying to survive. Another was a murder that Daisy thought no one knew about when she killed Cedric Tomlin in the V-12 night club with that silenced handgun and that threesome she did with Shayla Grimes and Man-Man just to manipulate information out of him to find PeeWee McMillan and set him on fire. Shadow then spoke of several more murders that Daisy and Von and Remmy did together when they thought they were alone. All these killings throughout the years, Shadow knew of, but what was even more shocking was that he had been playing in the shadows the whole time, watching her progress as a killer. It irked her to the point that if he really wanted to, Shadow could've killed her without anybody being the wiser, yet there she still stood, in the face of a man the streets knew nothing of but feared.

"Why me?" asked Daisy.

"You're not just the only one, Daisy. I have quite a few people I've had my eyes on. Ain't that right, daughter?" asked Shadow, casting his gaze over at Chloe standing across the room.

"Daughter?" Daisy stiffened.

Chloe shrugged with nonchalance. "Some thangs are better not known due to risk factors, Daisy. So now you know who I am."

"And why reveal this to me now, Shadow?"

"Amos," he corrected. "This is a sign of trust. And faith. I've been wantin' to bring you in the loop for a long time now, Daisy.

"Why?"

"Your track record. You're a remarkable killah – intelligent, fearless, and very respectable. And I want you to lead my new kill team into a prosperous unit."

"Your kill team?" Daisy remarked.

"Which consists of two others. Now that Von doesn't have her hooks in you any longer, I've decided to ask your hand in being my chief enforcer."

That was when he turned away from Daisy to step around the backside of the bed and dragged out a leather briefcase. He hefted the briefcase up and carried it over toward Daisy.

"Your initial payment is right here to do wit' as you please."

"A million dollars even," said Chloe, but Daisy also heard a little saltiness in her tone.

"A million bucks," he added.

"And who will I be workin' wit?"

"The two that I have mentioned."

"Who?" Daisy demanded, watching Chloe exit the room.

"Dolomite Thomas and Samantha Carmichael."

"Dolo and Sammy Jo."

Daisy knew them both very well and was fond of Sammy Jo. The bitch was a real deal smacker. She was beautiful and a little head-strong but nothing that Daisy couldn't handle if need be.

"Okay. You got me two of the best killaz. And what will be our first mission in order?"

"His name is Omar Andrade," said Shadow, who'd rather be called his government name while in daylight and outside of his comfort zone.

"Omar." Daisy knew him too. "Getting to him won't be easy. I'll tell you that."

"And that's why I chose you, Daisy. I like how you move. I'm sure you can manage. Now, do we have a deal?" Shadow extended his hand, and Daisy looked at it for a moment, then she took it and shook his hand in agreement.

"Deal," she said.

"Good."

…And then, Daisy came up swiftly with the scalpel and slit Shadow's throat from ear to ear.

"That's for killin' my father, muthafucker. You thought after all those years, I wouldn't remember your face? My father trusted you, that I remember as well. You setup the car accident that killed him. You're a master manipulator, Shadow. I've always known who you were, but I was just bidding my time before I killed you myself."

Shadow reached out to grab her, but Daisy sidestepped him with a mean right jab to his jaw. The killer tilted and hit the floor hard.

"Slippaz don't count," she said.

Sure enough, he had slipped up hard, thinking he could control Daisy with money and intelligence. All she did was use it against him, just like she knew Von's father was Cujo, another person responsible for her father's death all those years ago.

Calvin Dennis had been a great man of power and wealth before he allowed those he trusted the most to ruin him. Her whole life since her father's death had been spent living one lie after another, grooming herself into the person she was today, only to seek the vengeance she longed to do for so long now. Then, she approached the bed next. This would be easy. Killin' was her thing. Minutes later, Daisy was stepping into the elevator in her white lab coat and face mask and sunglasses with the briefcase in her hand – payment for all her hard work. It was ironic how things just worked out so well when you least expected it to.

Chapter 13

Keeping Pooh alive would be the worst mistake ever, so Ray and Qay gave her one shot to the head and dropped her out way out in the country of the Dog Town area on a secluded back road. During that time, Ray's good friend, Frank, visited the scene of the crime where Chad and Leo met their deaths. Being the true friend that he was, Frank Grant assessed the crime scene, interviewed witnesses, and then he did something he'd never done before. He destroyed all evidence implicating Ray of the crime. Without the videotape and the witness' testimonies, it would buy Ray enough time to get his shit together.

Frank knew his buddy was guilty, but he could not put himself to the task of seeing Ray go down – a true friend's honor. Meanwhile, Ray and Qay were headed back to the house where Rayneshia was. Qay stressed to his girl's father that he should be truthful with Rayneisha and tell her about Envy. Of course, Ray wasn't trying to hear that, but he knew Qay was right. He'd held the truth of Envy's existence for far too long now. It wasn't gonna be pretty, but he had to, and Ray was prepared for the hurt it would cause her. It was bad enough that Latrice was dead, and Rayneisha was heartbroken because of it. Then, the fact that she had another sibling would definitely be troubling as well.

On the ride to the house, Ray dwelled on the matter of how he should approach the subject. When he finally reached the house, there was another vehicle parked out front. A maroon colored Corvette was shining brilliantly under the sunshine. It was a car neither of them had seen before and all the more reason for them to get out and go see for themselves.

"I'm telling you now, son, if it ain't anybody that I approve of, I'm going in on them," said Ray, as he landed on the front doorstep.

Qay stepped right behind him as they entered. Then, Ray got the shock of his life when he found Bumpy Gilyard sitting on his living room sofa, puffing on a Cuban cigar. Standing on either side of him were two young shooters who already had their artillery at ready.

"Been waiting on you to show up, Ray," said Bumpy, the cousin of Latrice and a reputed gangster that Ray really didn't want any issues with. Before, he was relieved of that beast which had lived in him. Now, Ray didn't give two fucks how Bumpy felt about him now that Latrice was dead and gone.

"Where's my daughter?"

"I sent her away to deal wit' you."

"Deal wit' me?" Ray didn't like the sound of that.

Qay fished out his phone to call Rayneisha, unaffected by one of the young shooters lifting up his assault rifle to aim at him. Bumpy stood up, his short stature strongly built and attired in a Hugo Boss suit. Bumpy was from that old original gangsta era, not this new age bullshit like they had today.

"You was supposed to protect Latrice like you said you would, Ray," said Bumpy.

"It was too much going on for me to do so."

"Now this is going on, Ray." Bumpy snapped his fingers and out came two more gunmen from the kitchen doorway and the coat closet in the foyer behind Ray and Qay.

Ray didn't even flinch when one of the shooters pressed his Draco machine gun against his temple.

"If you think killin' me would solve anything, then you got the wrong idea, Bumpy."

"Killin' you is the least of my worries, Ray."

"Then what the fuck you want?"

"Because there's somebody else who'll find just as much pleasure in killin' you than me witnessin' it wit' a big smile on my face," Bumpy replied.

"Sup, nigga?!" Qay challenged the other gunman who initially sized him up and had his gun pointing at his body mass. "You don't put no fear in my heart, none whatsoever," he said.

"Tough. Arrogance. But stupid as hell," Bumpy said of Qay's character before turning his attention back on the man he came there for. "You remember Al Foster from HillSide, don't you?

"Sure do, Ray," said Bumpy. "Fifteen years is a long time to hold grudges, Ray."

No sooner than the words left his mouth did Al exit from the kitchen next with a meat cleaver in his hand. Qay looked at Ray in alarm.

Fifteen years ago, Al was sought after for the murders of Dr. Stacey Lambert and her husband in retaliation for Al's grandmother dying on the doctor's watch. Back then, Ray was transitioning to becoming a homicide detective and was assigned to Al's case. When Ray eventually located Al at a bar downtown to take him in for questioning, Al took off running but not before opening fire on Ray first. Ray took chase and stopped Al just out the rear exit of the bar by putting bullets into him from behind.

Al later went in for two counts of homicide, but the case got dismissed due to lack of evidence. He did go down for possession and attempted murder and assault on a law enforcement officer. He was still sentenced to twenty years, but there he stood among Ray some fifteen years later.

"Retaliation is a must, Ray," said Bumpy with a wicked smirk on his face.

"You brought this man into my house, Bumpy!"

Bumpy shrugged. "Of all thangs you could be saying right now, those are the words you chose to speak, Ray?" he replied.

That was when the blow struck Ray in the back of the head, knocking him out cold. Al grunted with pleasure. He was about to violate Ray in the worst way a man could ever be violated.

"You niggaz are some bitches," said Qay.

"Kill him," ordered Bumpy.

One swipe with the meat cleaver was all it took to put Qay down. Then, Al moved in on Ray.

***

There was one thing that Rayneisha wasn't, and that was a fool. She knew what the deal was when her older cousin, Bumpy, came knocking. He wanted to penalize her father for what happened to her mother, but Rayneisha couldn't allow him to do that. That was why she called Cody, and when he came, he came with an army of goons. It was then that she met Rikah and was introduced to the rest of the crew. A plan was put in motion. All they had to do was wait until Ray and Qay showed up to press play. By the time they arrived, the kill team was in position, while Rayneisha, Rikah, Cody, and Tuk oversaw the whole operation.

"It's action going on inside, y'all," said Rikah, having just been informed through her communicator by one of her men who was observing the situation inside the house.

"What type of action?" asked Rayneisha.

Rikah cut her eyes from Rayneisha to look at Cody.

"I'm bout to make that move now," she said before punching in the number to reach Bumpy.

In the backseat of the SUV they were occupying some ways down from the house, Rayneisha looked toward the house longingly.

"What's going on? Rikah? Talk to me, dammit!" she said wearily.

"Shhh. Bumpy, you already know who this is," said Rikah into the phone.

In the background, you could hear Ray screaming and raving like a madman through the phone. The cabin of the SUV was so quiet that even the others heard Ray's cries loud and clear. Rayneisha dropped her head and closed her eyes, as she fought the urge to get out and run to her father. Cody sensed this of his sister and reached over to take her hand into his and held on to it.

"Now is not the time, Rikah. Is this so detrimental that it can't be discussed later because as you can hear, I'm being quite entertained right now?" Bumpy said, and Rayneisha opened her mouth to have an outburst.

"No," Cody whispered to her.

Rikah said, "It is detrimental. Whatever you're doing to Ray right now must stop."

"What?"

"I shouldn't have to repeat myself, Bumpy."

A long pause ensued between them while Ray continued to release his pain in agony.

"Observe yourself and all the people around you right quick," said Rikah.

She didn't need to see it to know that infrared beams were dancing along the bodies of Bumpy and his men. Rikah had her shooters positioned like a SWAT team unit, surrounding the house from the outside with one man inside, having infiltrated Bumpy's inner circle by manipulation and good deeds to win him over.

"I'm impressed," said Bumpy. "I see the game has taught you well." He sounded enthusiastic about it.

"Why is Ray still hollerin'?"

"I have no control of that," said Bumpy. "A whole nother beast is in progress."

"You can stop it, Bumpy," she told him.

"I can't even if I tried."

With that being said, Rikah operated her communicator to send out her signal: Attack. Just like that, shots rang out from every direction, as bullets traveled through the air through windows and into the bodies of their targets – all except one.

"Move in," said Rikah. Then, she glanced back at Rayneisha and Cody and said, "C'mon."

One after the other, they exited the SUV, as the kill team rushed in on the house while guarding the premise at the same time. Rayneisha was running up the sidewalk toward her house. She was trying to get there to see her father.

As for Cody, he ran but not as hard as his sister was, but by the time he made it to the house and inside after her, he wished he had not even been there to witness it. The second he walked through the door, his sense of smell was assaulted by the stench of shit. He followed where the commotion was taking place and couldn't believe his eyes.

Bumpy had sicced Al on Ray while two of his men held him down and let Al rape him. The faggot ass nigga had ruined Ray. He couldn't even stand up; his pants had been ripped down to his ankles. Blood and shit permeated the entire house. Ray was still sobbing, as he laid there on the floor of the living room like a broken man.

All around them, dead bodies lay after being shot to death – everybody but Bumpy, who had taken two shots to each one of his legs. He was writhing around on the bloody floor in excruciating pain.

"You shoulda taken my warning," said Rikah, looking down at Bumpy in disgust.

Rayneisha was all over Qay, as he laid there dead from a chop of the meat cleaver to his neck. The sharp blade damn near severed his head and remained lodged in Qay's neck. It was awful. Then, that animalistic rage exploded from her, as Rayneisha snatched the meat cleaver from his neck in three tugs. Once the blade was free, instead of getting back up to her feet, Rayneisha crawled on her hands and knees across the floor to Bumpy. Then, she climbed on top of him and raised the meat cleaver with both hands over her head.

"It's all the way up now," said Tuk.

The meat cleaver swung downward and struck Bumpy in the middle of his face. Two powerful jerks to the blade and it came free again, and Rayneshia did not spare him any. She swung that bloody meat cleaver until blood blinded her vision, but she never dared to stop herself. The only thing that stopped her was her father's voice next to her. Then, he pulled her up into his arms. Ray could barely stand up straight, but he managed the task despite how painfully difficult it was.

"Time's up in here," said Rikah.

She then put in a call for the cleanup crew to swing by and do what they were good at. After a while, Cody watched from out front, as Rayneisha and their father exited the house. Rayneisha didn't look like herself, but Cody knew she would get through it.

"Phone's for you," said Rikah from the doorway of the SUV they'd rode in earlier.

Cody exchanged a look with her and stepped over to retrieve the phone from her. He gave her a questioning look, as he placed the phone to his ear. Behind them, two of Rikah's men argued back-and-forth about who was gonna drive the Corvette first. Behind the house was another couple of vehicles that Bumpy's shooters arrived in. It was all up for the taking.

"Who this?" Cody replied.

"It's me," came the voice of Ava, the twin sister of Avery.

It sounded like she'd been crying from the queasiness in her nasal tone. At hearing her voice, Cody said, "I love you, sista. And I promise you wit' everythang in me that I'm gon' deal wit' it, sis."

"We gon' deal wit' it, brotha. We," she said.

He froze.

"I'll be home in a few hours, Cody. I'm just waitin' on them to finish wit' the paperwork."

"But how? Didn't they give you twenty-one days…"

Ava cut him off and told him that after hearing about what was going on, she decided to do what her brother had done. But instead, she did it to one of the other girls in her housing unit that was bullying all the other girls around. Ava broke her face with an iron steel pipe she broke off the housing shower stall unit. By the time help came, the girl was already stretched out unconscious.

Ava was being processed at the local county jail under assault charges. A bond hearing would be conducted this afternoon via video session with the assigned county judge.

"When I get there, I won't have no understandin' about what happened to my brotha," said Ava, who was being judicated with a direct file procedure as being charged as an adult.

"I'll be waitin' for you," said Cody.

"Brah?" she called out to him.

"Yeah."

"I'm not fuckin' off," Ava replied.

Then, she disconnected and gave Cody the dial tone.

Chapter 14

The best thing that could have ever happened at that moment was when Ms. Donna showed up in Bebop's room. Tami wasted no time leaving the old lady there to watch over Bebop. Tami didn't want to leave her baby boy, but there were more pressing matters back home that demanded her presence.

Tami cried with her sister when she called to tell her that Avery was dead. Then, the hospital went on lockdown after what took place next door to Bebop's room. Two dead bodies in the room had the hospital in an uproar. The TPD officials were all over the building demanding answers. The first place they went was next door to Bebop's room where they found a list of people but no killer.

Besides, a credible physician was present in the room during the estimated time of death, which verified everybody's alibis in the room. The officials hated that, even the two goons Twan had summoned to the hospital to look after Tami. Brico and Kapo were two brothers who were licensed to carry a firearm, which irked the hell out of the two police detectives who came with the bullshit.

It was Brico who later claimed that he saw Daisy sneak into the room real sneaky like. She left out the way she came in, quiet as a mouse and swift like the wind. Tami had already figured one of her peoples were going to eventually slide up on Von's father and do it to him something fierce. Before exiting the building, Tami saw Manda in the vicinity, and they chopped it up for a while. Tami learned some things further of what was going on back home besides the notion that Rontay would never see the streets of Quincy again. He was upholding his code of silence, and even that didn't matter now with the concrete evidence they had against him. Tami didn't give a fuck about any of that. All she cared about was reaching home to be with her sistaz and locate her son. Then, Kapo received a call from somebody he knew in regard to someone name G-Mack and him being MIA now that his Gangsta Disciple brethren were aware of him being a snitch. Whoever this AP character was, Tami guessed he was the one pushing the buttons to get G-Mack killed. So, Kapo was to keep his eyes and ears open where G-Mack was concerned because he was officially living on borrowed time right now.

The drive back to Quincy was spent smoking Runtz weed and vibing out to rapper Lil Durk. To Tami, the music nowadays was whack! They didn't tell stories with powerful messages anymore. It was just not the type of music she herself could see herself bumping in her own ride. Nowadays, all it talked about was drill – meaning killin' niggaz for that paper or respect – damn. That was the main reason why everything was going to shits now.

Finally, when Tami made it to Pepper Hill. there were roadblocks everywhere, more killing, more drill! There was no place called safe now. Home didn't even feel like home anymore. Pepper Hill was a warzone, and it seemed to only get worse by the hour. After making a couple of phone calls, Tami learned that Ava was currently being picked up from the county jail by Felicia. Baby girl had followed in her twin brother's footsteps and was now about to raise pure hell over her dead brother.

Shequita wasn't picking up her phone, but Tami knew why, including where her sister might be at that moment if not home. Twan and Rod had also made it back in town, but the news Twan had for her made Tami want to break something.

"Take me to High Bridge," Tami said.

"Where that at?" asked Brico.

Tami thumped the side of her head.

"I forgot y'all ain't from around here. Just drive and I'll direct you, Brico," she told him.

About fifteen minutes later, they pulled up into the driveway of Rikah's childhood home. The house was now hers officially after buying her mother her dream house out in Midway. All types of cars were posted up out front, choppin it up and mingling amongst one another. Tami could feel the tension in the air way before she even stepped out of the car.

"Y'all got me so damn high it don't even feel like my damn feet is touchin' the ground," said Tami, letting herself in through the side entrance of the gate surrounding the house.

Kapo chuckled. "I got more where that came from wheneva you wanna go up again."

"I'm good on that, honey."

As she approached the front door of the house, it opened, and Cody stepped out onto the doorstep. Seeing her son made Tami put some pep in her step.

"We need to talk, Ma," Cody said.

"I know," Tami sighed.

Behind Cody, the door opened again, and then Stefani stepped outside next to him. At seeing this, Tami automatically knew that whoever this girl was, she had an effect on her son.

"Give me a minute wit' my mama, Stefani," said Cody then gestured for his mother to follow him.

He headed in the direction alongside the house where they could talk in peace.

"Is that your little girlfriend, Cody?"

"That's not important."

He didn't deny it, and that was all good with her. It was good to know that her son was interested in girls. For a while now, Tami had wondered whether his brothers were more important than his love life and of course Ava, who was interested in boys up until her brothers beat them up.

"I have a question to ask you, Ma," said Cody once they made it around back.

"You wanna know about me and Rodney?"

"That too," he replied. "But my question to you is this, Ma. How would you feel if I kill Teddy?" Cody's gaze was sharp and steady, and there was no questioning the seriousness in his tone.

"I heard he had something to do wit' Av getting killed in our house. Damn, baby. This shit is getting outta control now. Did you really kill Bizkit?" she asked, and Cody just looked at her like she'd offended him by asking him that. "Well, Cody, what's done can't be undone. It won't bring Av back. And I know how you feel about your brothas. Teddy is losing himself."

"I almost did it to Mel earlier," he said.

That really moved her. Money Mel was the only big brother the boys and Ava ever had, and for Cody to say what he said, things were definitely out of control. Then, Cody told her about the situation and what it led him into doing. Her son was committed, and who was Tami to tell him he was wrong? It was a war going on. No one was exempt.

"I know what I'm about to do; I can see you and Mama Quita fallin' out over it. Then, I still might have to kill Mel. Then, when Ava gets here, she's gonna turn up about Av, and I can't let nothin' happen to her too."

"Too? Baby, none of this is your fault." Tami reached out to stroke his arm.

"But it kinda is my fault."

"How so?"

"All this shit originated about a pair of shoes I felt you couldn't get me, and I had to do what I had to do to get the money and ended up being in the wrong place at the wrong time and look what transpired from it."

"I know."

Tami pulled her son into her arms. Cody resisted for a second, then his body awakened to his mother's affection. He hugged her back, as both of their hearts beat to the same rhythm.

"And I'm gonna burn our house down too."

Tami pulled away from him.

"What?"

"I'll buy you another house, Ma. I promise. When all this shit's over, I'ma get right on it. Even if I have to jack a muthafucker for their house to put you in it, I'ma do it."

"No!"

"I'm serious."

"And I know you are, baby. That's what scares me the most. That monster that's in you now. It only knows one thang," she told him.

"And what's that, Ma?"

Tami shook her head wearily. "Kill."

***

Rayneshia slapped her father so hard that Ray would have sworn he felt his back tooth come loose. He stared up at her and saw the fire in her eyes blazing with hurt and anger toward him. Ray was really taken aback when Rayneisha then pulled out the .9mm pistol Twan had given her earlier. He and Rikah made it clear that no one was to go unarmed, meaning Stefani, Pumpkin, and Maya, who was already strapped with the baby .380 automatic her big brother had given her.

At that moment, Rayneisha wanted to shoot her father in his fucking face. Ray had just confessed to her about Envy, and the truth of the matter hit her so hard that she wanted to hurt him. The crazy part was the fact that she and Envy were friends already. Envy owned the hair salon that Rayneisha frequented, and she had been acquainted with Envy for almost three years now.

"You ain't even worth shootin'," said Rayneisha, sneering at her father like a vicious hyena.

"I'm sorry. I was dead wrong..." he said.

"Fuck you, Ray!" Rayneisha pointed the gun back at him, growled loudly, then spun on her heels, and headed for the door of the bedroom.

Moments later, Rayneisha was storming up the hallway toward the ruckus going on up front. The big living room was filled with the bodies of Rikah and Twan's teams, Cody and his mother, plus Ray's main man, Frank, who rose up to his feet when he saw her. Frank had known Rayneisha since she was a little girl; he considered himself her uncle somewhat. It was evident Frank wanted to separate himself from all the killaz and gangstas in the room.

"What's wrong, Rayneisha?" asked Frank, seeing that look on her face, which meant trouble.

With the gun still in her hand, Rayneisha marched past Frank and the others for the front door. Cody saw this and stood up immediately, but Rayneisha wasn't trying to hear anything. She was in a dark place right now, so it was best to leave her be.

Then, Rayneisha snatched the front door open, and there stood Ava on the doorstep. For a brief moment, Rayneisha looked at Ava and recognized the resemblance to Avery. She didn't speak on it and just brushed past Ava, bumping her shoulder in the process.

"Bitch, watch where the fuck you going," snapped Ava.

Rayneisha stopped instantly and glared back over her shoulder at Ava before turning fully around to face her head on.

"*Bitch?!*" she said.

"That's what I said. Bitch. I'm supposed to be scared because you got a gun in your hand?"

A wicked smirk crossed Rayneisha's face. Then, she upped the .9mm and rushed toward Ava. Ava put her dukes up and stood in her fighting stance.

"Fall back, sis!" Cody suddenly appeared, stepping around Ava to put himself in between the two. "Not her, Rayneisha. Ava's family. This my sista," he replied.

"I'm your sista too, nigga!" Rayneisha retorted.

"What's going on?" Rikah intervened.

"Somebody need to show this bitch some manners before she get her ass spanked," said Ava.

"Who gon' spank me?"

"Me," Ava shrugged.

"Little gurl, you do not want none of this."

"Then put that gun down and let's see if you really can wallow, bitch."

"You got a death wish or somethin'?"

That was when Felicia stepped forward and asked them both to calm down. Felicia knew Rayneisha, having just met her the evening before. On their way there, Felicia had shared with Ava all the things that had transpired between their family and friends and the streets. She told Ava about Rayneisha; the thing was that Ava didn't know what Rayneisha looked like until now.

Ava glared at Rayneisha and said, "You got somethin' on your chest then get it off."

"I say let then thump," said Tator, one of the younger goons standing amongst the group in the yard.

"I agree," said Twan. "Get that shit off y'all chest because we don't need no animosity in our group. We are all a team now, and if anybody got it on their minds, then handle that shit like gangstas."

"You ain't said nothin'," Ava replied.

"Rayneisha?" Cody looked over at his sister.

Rayneisha handed her gun over to one of the fellas and turned for the front yard. There was nothing else that needed to be said. Rayneisha was down for some straightening; she needed to release some pressure. Cody came forward to meet Rayneisha.

"You better keep it clean too," he said.

"Don't talk to me right now, Cody."

Rayneisha cracked her knuckles, as she watched Ava come down the porch steps behind Cody. The guys created a circle in the yard, while Tami, Felicia, Twan, and Po' Boy stood off to the side to observe the situation. Felicia looked confident as to what her daughter could do in hand to hand combat. Ava was very skilled in that department.

"Y'all ready?" asked Rod.

Ava got in her fighting stance, looking like a younger version of Laila Ali.

"What're we waitin' on?" she said and moved toward Rayneisha.

Rayneisha was the first to throw a blow to which Ava weaved swiftly before connecting a quick jab to her jaw. For Rayneisha, fighting was like second nature to her, so she counterattacked with grace. Her next punch was avoided swiftly because Ava was smooth on her feet, but not the next two, which Ava took like a champ to the face. From there, a boxing match began, as both Rayneisha and Ava did their thing.

"Hmph." Felicia folded her arms, as she watched, knowing her daughter was holding out.

"Ava's bullshittin'," said Tami. "Look at her."

Ava was dancing all around her opponent, and it was clear that Rayneisha was getting frustrated with it. She was too fast and fought with stealth. Rayneisha decided to take the matter further and tried to wrestle her to the ground.

"Now, why do she wanna do that?" said Felicia.

Before anyone even realized what was happening, Rayneisha was screaming like a madwoman. Apparently, the ground game was what Ava did best. Thanks to her jujitsu training by her uncle and brother, Ava had somehow mastered her ground techniques. Where Rayneisha thought her heavier frame could work to her advantage to beat Ava on the ground, she had to find out the hard way that this was where Ava really wanted her. With no problem at all, Ava locked onto Rayneisha with a powerful arm-bar and leg-bar, dislocated her shoulder, and used her injury to thrash her ass like she stole something.

"Oh, no," muttered Rikah.

"Oh, yeah," said Felicia. "That's what she wanted, so that's what she gets."

Before Ava was allowed to pound Rayneisha to death, she backed away on her own and just stood there, staring down at Rayneisha. She was bloody and bruised and extremely humiliated. Ava shook her head and walked away into the house without a backward glance.

"I coulda killed her," she told Twan later, "but that's not who I want to do it to."

"Who then?" asked Twan.

"Teddy," she said. "I'm gonna kill Teddy."

You could see it in her eyes. There was nothing but blood in them for the boy she loved like a brother.

Chapter 15

Speaking of which, Teddy was teamed up with a third individual known as Lil Jessie. Lil Jessie was loyal to a fault, always ready to wreck something, but he was by far a pushover for Teddy and would pretty much do whatever Teddy said without question. To Teddy, he was just a tool to be used for what he had in mind. Then. he would have Ritchie murder him once he served his purpose. It was a dirty game. A cold world. Teddy had gotten wind that Tink Tink was released from the hospital the day before. Of all the dark thoughts that'd completely consumed him, the main one was killing Tink Tink. It was his top priority. Teddy felt as though he couldn't move on unless he sought vengeance on her. He wanted to do her something fierce, destroy her whole existence, and that was where Teddy was at the moment. All it took was a phone call that informed him that Tink Tink was currently at home under bedrest restrictions, so he was about to give her another rude awakening.

The three of them were parked up the street from where Tink Tink lived. When it was time to move, Teddy tapped the back of the driver seat. Lil Jessie nodded, and the stolen Camaro moved forward toward the beige and brownish colored house on Moore Road. A muthafucker was not about to be ready for what they were about to do.

A minute later, the Camaro swerved next to the curb outside the house in question. Then, Lil Jessie and Ritchie got out with them thangs on tuck and charged straight for the front door. Teddy took his time getting out the still idling car.

By the time he reached the front doorstep, his two goons had already forced themselves into the house. The instant he stepped through the front door, Teddy heard a woman scream. The scream came from the kitchen where Ritchie already had Tink Tink's mother, Jill, face down on the floor. "Where she at?" Teddy asked.

Then, that was where he heard the struggle down the hallway. That was where Lil Jessie was, and he was tussling with Tink Tink in her bedroom. When Teddy appeared in the doorway, Tink Tink looked up and gasped in horror. Lil Jessie took that second to slam her into the floor of the bedroom.

"Noo," Tink Tink cried when she saw Teddy draw the box cutter he had in his pants pocket.

Then, he made his way toward her all slow and creepy-like.

"Payback is a bitch, bitch!" said Teddy, his scarred face a hideous mask of murderous intentions.

For the next minute or two, while Lil Jessie held her down, Teddy sliced her face to ribbons. Then, he used that same blade to butcher her tongue and gouge out both of her eyeballs before finally pressing his gun to her forehead and pulling the trigger. Blood was all over the room and Teddy's clothes, and as for Lil Jessie, he was stunned by what he had just witnessed.

"Damn, brah. You did some beast-mode shit just then," he told Teddy, who tugged his fitted cap lower over his shades and exited the room.

Minutes later, after Ritchie killed the mother by strangulation, they were back in traffic like nothing happened, but before they could get far, a patrol unit hit the lights behind them. This time, Ritchie was behind the wheel, and he told everybody to remain calm.

"What you fixin' to do, brah?" asked Teddy.

"I'm pullin' over," said Ritchie.

"You doing what?!" Lil Jessie bellowed.

Ritchie told Lil Jessie to just chill, not to panic, that he had everything under control, and so, he pulled the car over alongside Atlanta Street. Behind them, there were two cops in the car.

"You already know what's about to go down, brah. I ain't doing no talkin' or getting out the car. I'm 'bout to blast on these muthafuckas," said Ritchie, his pistol already cocked and ready to do some damage.

In the back seat, Teddy scooted over to his right, closer to the door. The window was down already, plus Teddy never put away his gun, but he did pull out the second firearm which was a Beretta .9mm that was a favorite of Bizkit's.

"Let's rock 'em to sleep then," said Teddy.

"They getting out now," Lil Jessie announced from his side mirror observation.

Sure enough, both policemen removed themselves from their cruiser. One was a Black, older guy with a crew cut. The younger, white cop was slender built, bald headed, and coming up on Teddy's right side, but they both had their hands on their sidearms, as they made their approach on either side of the car.

"This shit crazy, man," Lil Jessie replied nervously.

"Shut the fuck up, Jessie!" said Ritchie through clenched teeth.

Out of the corner of his eye, he watched Lil Jessie remove his pistol just as the white cop was just in front of the back passenger door. That was when Lil Jessie panicked, swung the passenger door open, bolted from the car with his gun up. and then squeezed off one round before the much quicker cop cleared his holster and punched Lil Jessie with two slugs to the chest. Then, all of a sudden, Teddy was dumping rounds into the cop from the open window. Ritchie had his man where he wanted him and shot him four times, knocking him into moving traffic. A Jeep truck slammed into the cop with a powerful, sickening thud as body collided with metal.

It was an ugly sight, but there was no time to stay back and watch the rest.

Ritchie put the car back in gear just as Lil Jessie threw himself across the passenger seat.

"Help me, brah!" Lil Jessie cried out. "I'm shot!"

"Aight." Teddy leaned over the back of the passenger seat and dumped three rounds into Lil Jessie's head. "You dead now," he said.

The Camaro swung into traffic, as Lil Jessie's body, hanging halfway out of the passenger door, slowly dragged itself out into the now life-threatening traffic, and once again, this time, another cop car hit its sirens just as the Camaro shot past it. The police car turned into the path behind it and proceeded to pursue the Camaro.

"Shit!"

"You better drive this muthafucker, Ritchie!" said Teddy. "Or we both are dead," he added.

Ritchie punched the gas and went berserk in traffic. It was do or die time. Survival of the fittest.

***

"Oh, my Lord! Oh, God almighty Jesus, please don't let them kill my baby boy," cried Shequita, her eyes glued to the TV screen in her own living room.

On the TV was a live viewing of one of the longest and deadliest car chases in Quincy history. For going on thirty minutes now, the surveillance helicopter flying above had been recording the live footage of the chase. Prior to being alerted to officially assist with the car chase, the helicopter was summoned to another area where another supposed cop killer was on the run but on feet. But that was what you had the K-9 unit for, so the helicopter was dispatched to officialize the viewing of the live car chase. As the news commentator described the scene to the world, the actual viewing of the Camaro being chased by a dozen or so police cars was in progress. Looking at this shit in real life reminded you of that scene where Cleo and her crew from the movie, *Set It Off*, took the police on a high-speed chase through the city, but this one was more to a different angle than in the movie because the Camaro had long ago crossed the state lines into Georgia from the backway of Havana on Highway 27. The chase went from Quincy to Tallahassee and back toward Gadsden County where Ritchie zoomed through Havana to finally make their way through Valdosta now. Their only problem was that bird in the air; Ritchie couldn't shake that helicopter for nothing.

Sitting in front of the TV, crying her eyes out and on the verge of cardiac arrest, Shequita knew it was over with for her son. The next thing she knew, Money Mel came bursting through the front door with Po' Boy and some others behind them. Money Mel had his cell phone in his hand and had been watching the action take place there.

"Ma." Money Mel slid onto the sofa beside her.

"He called me," cried Shequita.

"He called you when?"

"Now. Then. While they was chasing them." Shequita pointed at the TV screen with a shaky hand. "He called to tell me he was sorry and that he loved me," she said wearily.

When she said this, Money Mel dropped his head in silent distress. When Teddy made the phone call, he believed in his heart that he was not gonna make it out alive. Teddy just wanted his last words to be to his mother, telling her how much he loved her before he went. That shit hurt Money Mel to the core. Teddy knew he was doomed, and losing his little brother was the last thing he wanted.

"C'mon. lil brah, beat 'em crackaz!" said Money Mel, rooting for his brother.

The newswoman from the state of Georgia was broadcasting every moment of the event, as Teddy and Ritchie's faces were plastered upon the top left corner of the TV screen. That was when it happened, the sudden moment of their fates. The Camaro suddenly jerked left, swerved right, then the vehicle spun out of control before it began to flip continuously, going at the speed of one hundred miles per hour. After about the fifth full flip of the car, a body was seen flying out from the Camaro and sliding across the ground of the pavement.

"Noo!" Shequita covered her eyes as she screamed.

Money Mel said, "Somebody turn that shit off. It's okay, Mama. It's a'ight." He pulled his mother into his arms while she kept screaming and crying, and Money Mel was trying to keep his composure too.

Po' Boy found the remote control and shut the TV off.

"Everybody outside," he said. "Now!"

There were only three others: Vega, Tyrone, and Pookey, and they trickled out the front door with Po' Boy in tow. It was best that Money Mel share that moment with his mother. They both needed one another, as the agony and pain from Teddy's demise rocked their whole world. His death would not only bring heartache but a vengeance that was like no other. Money Mel and his mother cried together. The last time he remembered sharing tears with his mother was when his grandmother, Liz, died. Shequita screamed her poor heart out; her pain – a mother's sorrow – was the worst ever. Her fears had been brought to reality with her baby boy's death. All she saw was a body being thrown from that car, and Shequita was dying inside.

The ring of Money Mel's cell phone didn't budge him, as he held his grieving mother. After about another twenty minutes, Shequita's pain and sorrow drained her of all her energy, and Money Mel laid her down upon the couch. She'd cried herself into exhaustion.

"I love you, Mama," Money Mel whispered before placing a gentle kiss upon her cheek, then he kissed her on her forehead and stood up.

Next, Money Mel made his way down the hall toward Teddy's bedroom. The door was ajar, as he pushed it open

120

fully and just stood there in the bedroom doorway, staring longingly inside.

"I was the one who was supposed to go first," said Money Mel. "Not you, lil brah."

He wanted to enter the room so bad, but a powerful force prevented him from going inside. A lone tear fell down his cheek.

"I love you, my nigga. Now, I'ma go even harder now, for both of us."

A few minutes later, Money Mel found himself stepping outside for some fresh air. Sitting on the porch steps, Po' Boy gazed up over his shoulder at him. Tyrone was the only one accompanying Po' Boy, while the other two were somewhere off doing God knows what.

"I got Auntie BaeBae handlin' the funeral arrangements for now. I know y'all need some time to get yourselves together. But you can holla at her wheneva you feel up to it," said Po' Boy.

Without a word, Money Mel moved forward to take a seat down on the porch step beside his homie. Tyrone pulled out a pre-rolled blunt of Kush and blazed it up before offering it to Money Mel.

"They just found out about Tink Tink and her mama," said Po' Boy.

No response from Money Mel.

"What I heard, brah had did that girl something dirty, so be prepared for the bullshit them crackaz gon' be servin' our way. Another one to two of them pigs don' got killed, and they gon' try and pull some shady shit on us to retaliate," added Po' Boy.

"Then they gonna get the bizness too," said Tyrone, already knowing what Money Mel's response would be.

Money Mel smoked the blunt without comment. He was drowning in grief, so distraught he wanted to scream. His baby brother was dead, and it would be a helluva pain to get over – if he ever got over it at all for that matter.

From up the street came two police cruisers and a black on black Chevy Suburban truck at the lead. The big truck was moving at an unhurried pace that let on that the person who was driving was searching for something. Searching for what? Who? Was it Money Mel due to what his brother did or just who he was entirely? The three-vehicle motorcade came to a sudden stop right in front of Shequita's house. At first, no one removed themselves from either vehicle. Then, the driver door of the truck opened, and Police Chief Moore pulled himself out of the big SUV. When Money Mel saw who it was, he stood up, and Po' Boy rose up to his feet at once.

"Looks like we bout to give these crackaz the bizness sooner than expected," Tyrone said. He was about to reach for his weapon, but Po' Boy told him to stand down for right now.

Chief Moore was closing the truck's door when both police car doors opened. Four policemen got out, and the chief shook his head no to them. He stepped over amongst the group and spoke to them in a tone the others couldn't hear.

"Here he goes," said Tyrone, watching as the other cops shot menacing daggers in their direction.

"Mel," stated Chief Moore, "if you don't mind, I'd like to talk to your motha."

"Right now ain't the time, cuz. You know what's going on. My brotha is dead; my mama lost her son. She's hurtin', man. So fall back."

"Who told you your brotha was dead, Mel?" said the older man who looked like he would rather be anywhere in the world but there facing Money Mel after all he'd been accused of doing.

"I saw it myself."

"The live footage on the news?"

Money Mel nodded.

The Chief of Police said, "The guy that was thrown from the car wasn't Teddy. That was Ritchie, but Teddy is indeed alive still." Chief Moore saw Money Mel reel back in astonishment at that statement and clenched his fists. "But he's in severe critical condition, Mel. He might not make it in the state he's in, and I'm tellin' you this outta confidence."

"Where my brotha at, nigga?" hissed Money Mel.

"I'm not at liberty to say, Mel. And even if I did, you won't be able to get to him. He's considered a menace to society. A shoot to kill order is in, and no one would be able to touch him."

"They'll kill my brotha anyway," said Money Mel. "And you know that shit, nigga."

"It's outta my hands now," said Chief Moore.

That was when Po' Boy spoke up, offering his opinion that if Teddy was to survive, he would be brought back to Quincy to stand before a judge.

"That is true," said the chief just before the front door opened, and Shequita stared out at them with bloodshot red eyes of sorrow.

Shequita stood there with one of Money Mel's guns in her possession.

"Mama," Money Mel turned toward his mother, "this nigga said Teddy ain't dead."

"I heard him," she said. Then, she upped the cannon and aimed it dead at the chief's head. "Now you gon' tell me where my son is."

Chapter 16

The sound of someone knocking on the front door interrupted Lauryn from her task of prepping for an early dinner with a friend. She brushed her hands into an apron and took another sip of her wine before heading to the door. Standing outside of the doormat was the last person Lauryn expected to see. After peering out the side window to identify the visitor, Lauryn reached for the door to open it.

"Daisy," she replied in surprise.

"I'm only going to be a minute, Lauren. I'm just tryna shake somebody right now."

"Shake who, Daisy?"

"The Feds," she said. "Gotta get 'em off my trail."

Lauryn gasped. "The FBI!" she blurted. "Are they watchin' my house right now? Like right now this second?" asked Lauryn, astounded by the whole thing.

"They are, Lauryn. I'm sorry."

"But why… Oh. Vontoria." Lauryn gave a sullen look at the thought of her employer being beheaded.

She knew Von to be a hard individual, one of the best at what she did, but never in a million years would Lauryn have imagined that happening.

Lauryn worked as a caregiver at the downtown daycare nursery that Von owned. She was actually the nursery's supervisor but was enjoying her much needed vacation. It was her first day off to be exact, and Lauryn was expecting to share it with her new man, Bernard.

"I got so much on my plate right now, and I gotta lose him if I'm to accomplish what I need to accomplish, Lauryn."

Daisy told her about the situation back at her place and where she felt Terrell's involvement was motivated by immodest intentions.

"You think he'll set you up?"

"People like Terrell is more loyal to his job than he is to anything or anybody."

"But he killed those men in cold blood."

"Which makes him all the more dangerous to trust, Lauryn. Yes, he killed them niggaz. And when his people showed up, his influence on them is why I'm not in custody right now. I believe Terrell saved me for his own personal gain."

"Which is?" Lauryn asked curiously.

"That's the point, Lauryn. I don't know."

The doorbell rang, and Lauryn was up and hurrying to go see who it was. Daisy remained where she was standing. If it was Terrell or any of his people, then she would have some words with them that just might provoke violence. They would just have to kill her today because she'd be damned if she allowed them to intimidate her.

"Daisy, it's my niece and nephew," said Lauryn before she opened the front door.

It was who walked through the door moments later that instantly brought Daisy to alertness. It was Yellow, and in his arms was his little sister, Eboni. She was asleep with her curly little head resting on his shoulder. When Yellow looked up and saw Daisy standing there, he came to an immediate halt. Then, instantly, he drew his pistol and paused, glancing from his sleeping baby sister back to Daisy.

"What's going on?" Lauryn looked from Daisy to her brother's son.

She didn't wait for an answer and reached for Eboni at once.

"I don't know what you got going on in here, Dee, but you shouldn't be here," he said.

Yellow looked like he hadn't slept in ages. There were dark bags under his red eyes. He looked like someone who was constantly on the run and not getting his proper rest. The nigga looked exhausted.

"I was just leaving anyway," said Daisy.

He just stood there, watching her.

"I don't give a damn what y'all do. Just don't upset my sweet pea," Lauryn replied, referring to Eboni by the pet name she'd given her. Then, she walked out of the room, leaving them alone.

Daisy said, "You the last one left, Yellow."

"That's what you think," he answered evenly.

"I know this for a fact."

He frowned. "I should kill you right now. You went against the grain. You sided wit' the enemy, and in my book, that's foul, my nigga."

"I sided wit' my family, my own flesh and blood, and Von knew this," she said.

Yellow was shaking his head.

"Avery wasn't family, Dee. He doesn't count. You betrayed us by saving him, knowing what he did to Pop Vince. Then, you sold out your sista to them niggaz..." He aimed his pistol at her face with his finger curled around the trigger. "You killed her," he growled.

"She killed herself, Yellow."

"That's because you made her do it by tellin' them niggaz about Shyleek."

She didn't deny that. She did have Von sacrifice her life for her son's, but Daisy was seeing something else at that moment, something she hadn't perceived up until now. She looked at Yellow, and it was clear as day.

"You loved her, didn't you?"

Yellow froze at her words.

"You know I did."

"You was in love wit' Von. I see it in your eyes." She saw it just like she saw Yellow shooting her dead right there in the living room.

It didn't scare Daisy; she was more mad at herself for slippin' like that. Then, he pulled the trigger, shooting Daisy twice in the chest. She spun from the impact and fell face first into the floor. Then, Yellow took two steps forward to put one in her head, but the sudden cries of his little sister calling out for him brought him short of doing it.

"Eboni! I'm here. I'm coming!" Yellow called out to her and tucked his weapon away, as he raced from the living room down the hall.

Moments later, Lauryn came running into the living room, and when she saw Daisy, she gasped and touched her heart. Then, she turned around and ran back down the hallway. That was when it was heard that Lauryn was telling him about the possibility that Daisy was followed there to the house.

By this time, Daisy was back up on her feet and staring down at the bulletproof vest she was wearing. She groaned and hissed in tremendous pain, as she touched the areas in which she had been shot. Yellow tried to kill her, and it was all because of the love he had for Von. His loyalty to her, even in death, was commendable and worthy to be praised. Then, Daisy finally drew her own weapon and moved in Yellow's direction. Eboni was still having a fit, while Lauryn and her nephew conversed in raised voices over the child.

Daisy was two feet from the bedroom door and a second from killing Yellow when she heard his intentions. He was telling his aunt about leaving the streets alone to raise Shyleek and Eboni. That was his vow to Von before she died, so he was going to get Shyleek back and then take him and Eboni somewhere safe and raise them on his own. For some reason, that shit touched Daisy almost more than the pain she was experiencing. The shit made her feel guilty. Then, she turned around and walked away and out of the front door, leaving it open.

By the time Yellow made it back in the front and saw that Daisy was gone, he already knew how she had survived those shots.

"Damn," he whispered angrily. "I shoulda popped that bitch in the head."

Epilogue

All it was about was a pair of shoes. If Cody hadn't taken it upon himself to go out and earn his keep, he wouldn't have become the victim of his own environment. He was better just watching it all from his front porch. When the smoke cleared, all that were left to pick up the pieces were Cody, Ava, Twan, and Rikah. No one knew where Daisy had run off to. While they struggled to uphold one another, Daisy was off in a whole other world that she would soon deem her own.

Meanwhile, Cody was labeled the new prince of the streets and with that position came a whole lot of responsibility, like keeping Ava close after what she did to earn her respect. Ava murdered both Money Mel and Po' Boy by throwing a pipe bomb into the car with them one evening. Her vengeance for what Teddy did to Avery had been an ongoing problem in the streets, always ready to pop off, but only a few could control her. That was Cody and Rayneisha, another person who had experienced a dramatic change in her life.

Rayneisha no longer wanted to be committed to a street nigga. Losing Qay was a pain so heavy on her that she couldn't breathe. Plus, Cody and her new brotha were enough street niggaz in her life as it was, but she and Cody did eventually meet Envy. Although the meeting was awkward, come to find out, Envy was very influential. Envy owned a bar, a catering business, a team of girls who boosted merch for a living and even tied in some heavy hittaz in the streets. Overall, their relationship was solidified by trust and loyalty to one another. As for Ray, the nigga ended up getting caught by the Feds trying to leave the country. Now, he was set to stand trial, and from what it looked like, Ray would die in prison.

Bebop was now confined to a wheelchair for the rest of his life. The little knucklehead was brave and so respectable that he had the whole streets of Gadsden County rooting for him. Rayneisha and Tami fussed over him all the time, awaiting word from the specialist who claimed he may have something that would help Bebop. He had the best doctors looking into his situation. Cody saw that his little brother received the best treatment, and if there was any mishap, he would punish them.

Twan was still growing in his pain over Alisha's death. He and Menace and Rod were back together again and leaning on one another for moral support through the hustle and Menace's sudden change for the worst character. Losing Alisha made him go into a dark mode that not even the devil himself wanted any parts of. They did visit Stockbridge, Georgia where they met Kordae Oliver, the man who knew her as Temica Davis – the husband who adored her endlessly and raised their son, Khalani, on his own while she juggled her double life. Alisha was a good woman; she just wanted to be different, to love, to give love, and leave her legacy to be respected.

Then, you had Rontay, now a critical informant for the police. Pressure burst pipes, and he could only hold onto his integrity for so long. Rontay told everything and on everybody. Cody and Twan were snatched up four times over the course of a month, but they remained firm and didn't allow themselves to be intimidated. They so badly wanted to make an example out of Cody, but somehow, he slipped through the cracks every time.

Yellow left the city after taking Shy and finding a nice spot out in Memphis where his female cousin, Dominque, lived and worked as a stewardess for the airlines. Now, Shy and Eboni were living in comfort but still affected by the tragedies of their latest extremities. Yellow was determined to give then a better life – no matter how much of a challenge Shy was. Before he called it quits, he would make the child grow up to love, respect, and appreciate him.

At last, Cody was where he wanted to be all along, a place where he would have meaning and purpose. He had to take some hard losses to get there, but he was determined to prevail. He was destined for greatness. It was his legacy to build now that he was. If only he never left the porch...

The End

Lock Down Publications and Ca$h Presents
Assisted Publishing Packages

Due to an increase in the price of services we have increased our prices. The prices below reflect the price increase as of 11/1/24.

BASIC PACKAGE	UPGRADED PACKAGE
$699	**$1000**
Editing	Typing
Cover Design	Editing
Formatting	Cover Design
	Formatting
	Upload eBooks to Amazon
	Upload Paperback to Amazon
ADVANCE PACKAGE	**LDP SUPREME PACKAGE**
$1,400	**$1,700**
Typing	Typing
Editing (line editing/content)	Editing (line editing/content)
Cover Design	Cover Design
Formatting	Formatting
Copyright Registration	Copyright Registration
Proofreading	Proofreading
Upload eBooks to Amazon	Set up Amazon Account
Upload Paperback to Amazon	Upload eBooks to Amazon
	Upload Paperback to Amazon
	Advertise on LDP's Amazon and Facebook Page

***
Other services available upon request.
Additional charges may apply

Lock Down Publications
P.O. Box 944
Stockbridge, GA 30281-9998
Phone: 470 303-9761
Email: lockdownpublications@gmail.com

132

Submission Guideline

Submit the first three chapters of your completed manuscript to ldpsubmissions@gmail.com. In the subject line add **Your Book's Title**. The manuscript must be in a Word Doc file and sent as an attachment. Document should be in Times New Roman, double spaced, and in size 12 font. Also, provide your synopsis and full contact information. If sending multiple submissions, they must each be in a separate email.

Have a story but no way to send it electronically? You can still submit to LDP/Ca$h Presents. Send in the first three chapters, written or typed, of your completed manuscript to:

LDP: Submissions Dept
P.O. Box 944
Stockbridge, GA 30281-9998

DO NOT send original manuscript. Must be a duplicate.
Provide your synopsis and a cover letter containing your full contact information.

Thanks for considering LDP and Ca$h Presents.

NEW RELEASES

BLOODLINE OF A SAVAGE 1-3
THESE VICIOUS STREETS 1-3
RELENTLESS GOON 1-3
BY PRINCE A. TAUHID

THE BUTTERFLY MAFIA 1-3
BY FUMIYA PAYNE

A THUG'S STREET PRINCESS 1&2
BY MEESHA

CITY OF SMOKE 3
BY MOLOTTI

GET IT IN SLUGS 1 &2
BY B. STALL

STANDING ON HER BUSINESS 1&2
BY DG SANTANA

STEPPERS 1,2&3
THE REAL BADDIES OF CHI-RAQ
BY KING RIO

THE LANE 1&2
BY KEN-KEN SPENCE

THUG OF SPADES 1&2
LOVE IN THE TRENCHES 2
CORNER BOYS
BY COREY ROBINSON

TIL DEATH 3
BY ARYANNA

THE BIRTH OF A GANGSTER 4
BY DELMONT PLAYER

PRODUCT OF THE STREETS 1-3
BY DEMOND "MONEY" ANDERSON

NO TIME FOR ERROR
BY KEESE

MONEY HUNGRY DEMONS 1-2
BY TRANAY ADAMS

HUB CITY MENACE 1-3
BY J. WHITE

A THUGGISH PASSION 1&2
LAND OF DA HOOLIGANZ 1-4
KILLAZ ON STANDBY 1&2
BY IRA B.

FO'EVA ROLLIN 1&2
BY ASSA RAYMOND BAKER

THE LEVEL UP 1&3
BY LUXURY KING

Coming Soon from Lock Down Publications/Ca$h Presents

IF YOU CROSS ME ONCE 6
ANGEL V
By Anthony Fields

A THUGS STREET PRINCESS 3
By Meesha

CORNER BOYS 2
By Corey Robinson

THA TAKEOVER
By Keith Chandler

BETRAYAL OF A G 2
By Ray Vinci

SAVAGE FAMILY EMPIRE 1&2
SOULLESS GOON 1,2&3
THE DIRTY SIDE OF MONEY 1,2&3
By Prince

FOR MY ENEMY'S SAKE
AMBITIONS OF A SLIDER
FRESH OFF DA PORCH
By IRA B.

THE TRUCKLOAD 1-4
TIPPIN' THE SCALES 1-3
BAD BITCHES WIT GUNZ 3
PROBLEM SOLVED 2
By Christopher "Diesel" Hornezes

Available Now

RESTRAINING ORDER 1 & 2
By **CA$H & Coffee**

LOVE KNOWS NO BOUNDARIES 1-3
By **Coffee**

RAISED AS A GOON I, II, III & IV
BRED BY THE SLUMS I, II, III
BLAST FOR ME I & II
ROTTEN TO THE CORE I II III
A BRONX TALE I, II, III
DUFFLE BAG CARTEL I II III IV V VI
HEARTLESS GOON I II III IV V
A SAVAGE DOPEBOY I II
DRUG LORDS I II III
CUTTHROAT MAFIA I II
KING OF THE TRENCHES
By **Ghost**

LAY IT DOWN I & II
LAST OF A DYING BREED I II
BLOOD STAINS OF A SHOTTA I & II III
By **Jamaica**

LOYAL TO THE GAME I II III
LIFE OF SIN I, II III
By **TJ & Jelissa**

IF LOVING HIM IS WRONG…I & II
LOVE ME EVEN WHEN IT HURTS I II III
By **Jelissa**

PUSH IT TO THE LIMIT
By **Bre' Hayes**

BLOODY COMMAS I & II
SKI MASK CARTEL I, II & III
KING OF NEW YORK I II, III IV V
RISE TO POWER I II III
COKE KINGS I II III IV V
BORN HEARTLESS I II III IV
KING OF THE TRAP I II
By **T.J. Edwards**

WHEN THE STREETS CLAP BACK I & II III
THE HEART OF A SAVAGE I II III IV
MONEY MAFIA I II
LOYAL TO THE SOIL I II III
By **Jibril Williams**

A DISTINGUISHED THUG STOLE MY HEART I II & III
LOVE SHOULDN'T HURT I II III IV
RENEGADE BOYS 1-4
PAID IN KARMA 1-3
SAVAGE STORMS 1-3
AN UNFORESEEN LOVE 1-3
BABY, I'M WINTERTIME COLD 1-3
A THUG'S STREET PRINCESS 1&2
By **Meesha**

A GANGSTER'S CODE 1-3
A GANGSTER'S SYN 1-3
THE SAVAGE LIFE 1-3
CHAINED TO THE STREETS 1-3
BLOOD ON THE MONEY 1-3
A GANGSTA'S PAIN 1-3
BEAUTIFUL LIES AND UGLY TRUTHS
CHURCH IN THESE STREETS
By **J-Blunt**

CUM FOR ME 1-8
An LDP Erotica Collaboration

FRESH OFF DA PORCH 3 | IRA B.

BLOOD OF A BOSS 1-5
SHADOWS OF THE GAME
TRAP BASTARD
By **Askari**

THE STREETS BLEED MURDER 1-3
THE HEART OF A GANGSTA 1-3
By **Jerry Jackson**

WHEN A GOOD GIRL GOES BAD
By **Adrienne**

THE COST OF LOYALTY 1-3
By **Kweli**

BRIDE OF A HUSTLA 1-3
THE FETTI GIRLS 1-3
CORRUPTED BY A GANGSTA 1-4
BLINDED BY HIS LOVE
THE PRICE YOU PAY FOR LOVE 1-3
DOPE GIRL MAGIC 1-3
By **Destiny Skai**

A KINGPIN'S AMBITION
A KINGPIN'S AMBITION II
I MURDER FOR THE DOUGH
By **Ambitious**

TRUE SAVAGE 1-7
DOPE BOY MAGIC 1-3
MIDNIGHT CARTEL 1-3
CITY OF KINGZ 1&2
NIGHTMARE ON SILENT AVE
THE PLUG OF LIL MEXICO 1&2
CLASSIC CITY
By **Chris Green**

A GANGSTER'S REVENGE 1-4
THE BOSS MAN'S DAUGHTERS 1-5
A SAVAGE LOVE 1&2
BAE BELONGS TO ME 1&2
A HUSTLER'S DECEIT 1-3
WHAT BAD BITCHES DO 1-3
SOUL OF A MONSTER 1-3
KILL ZONE
A DOPE BOY'S QUEEN 1-3
TIL DEATH 1-3
IMMA DIE BOUT MINE 1-6
DYING FOR LIKES
By **Aryanna**

A DOPEBOY'S PRAYER
By **Eddie "Wolf" Lee**

THE KING CARTEL 1-3
By **Frank Gresham**

THESE NIGGAS AIN'T LOYAL 1-3
By **Nikki Tee**

GANGSTA SHYT 1-3
By **CATO**

THE ULTIMATE BETRAYAL
By **Phoenix**

BOSS'N UP 1-3
By **Royal Nicole**

I LOVE YOU TO DEATH
By **Destiny J**

I RIDE FOR MY HITTA
I STILL RIDE FOR MY HITTA
By **Misty Holt**

LOVE & CHASIN' PAPER
By **Qay Crockett**

TO DIE IN VAIN
SINS OF A HUSTLA
By **ASAD**

BROOKLYN HUSTLAZ
By **Boogsy Morina**

BROOKLYN ON LOCK 1 & 2
By **Sonovia**

GANGSTA CITY
By **Teddy Duke**

A DRUG KING AND HIS DIAMOND 1-3
A DOPEMAN'S RICHES
HER MAN, MINE'S TOO 1&2
CASH MONEY HO'S
THE WIFEY I USED TO BE 1&2
PRETTY GIRLS DO NASTY THINGS
By **Nicole Goosby**

LIPSTICK KILLAH 1-3
CRIME OF PASSION 1-3
FRIEND OR FOE 1-3
By **Mimi**

TRAPHOUSE KING 1-3
KINGPIN KILLAZ 1-3
STREET KINGS 1&2
PAID IN BLOOD 1&2
CARTEL KILLAZ 1-3
DOPE GODS 1&2
By **Hood Rich**

THE STREETS ARE CALLING
By **Duquie Wilson**

STEADY MOBBN' 1-3
THE STREETS STAINED MY SOUL 1-3
By **Marcellus Allen**

WHO SHOT YA 1-3
SON OF A DOPE FIEND 1-4
HEAVEN GOT A GHETTO 1&2
SKI MASK MONEY 1&2
By **Renta**

GORILLAZ IN THE BAY 1-4
TEARS OF A GANGSTA 1/&2
3X KRAZY 1&2
STRAIGHT BEAST MODE 1&2
By **DE'KARI**

TRIGGADALE 1-3
MURDA WAS THE CASE 1-3
By **Elijah R. Freeman**

SLAUGHTER GANG 1-3
RUTHLESS HEART 1-3
By **Willie Slaughter**

GOD BLESS THE TRAPPERS 1-3
THESE SCANDALOUS STREETS 1-3
FEAR MY GANGSTA 1-5
THESE STREETS DON'T LOVE NOBODY 1-2
BURY ME A G 1-5
A GANGSTA'S EMPIRE 1-4
THE DOPEMAN'S BODYGAURD 1&2
THE REALEST KILLAZ 1-3
THE LAST OF THE OGS 1-3
By **Tranay Adams**

MARRIED TO A BOSS 1-3
By **Destiny Skai & Chris Green**

KINGZ OF THE GAME 1-7
CRIME BOSS 1-4
By **Playa Ray**

FUK SHYT
By **Blakk Diamond**

DON'T F#CK WITH MY HEART 1&2
By **Linnea**

ADDICTED TO THE DRAMA 1-3
IN THE ARM OF HIS BOSS
By **Jamila**

LOYALTY AIN'T PROMISED 1&2
By **Keith Williams**

YAYO 1-4
A SHOOTER'S AMBITION 1&2
BRED IN THE GAME
By **S. Allen**

TRAP GOD 1-3
RICH $AVAGE 1-3
MONEY IN THE GRAVE 1-3
CARTEL MONEY 1&2
By **Martell Troublesome Bolden**

FOREVER GANGSTA 1&2
GLOCKS ON SATIN SHEETS 1&2
By **Adrian Dulan**

TOE TAGZ 1-4
LEVELS TO THIS SHYT 1&2
IT'S JUST ME AND YOU
By **Ah'Million**

KINGPIN DREAMS 1-3
RAN OFF ON DA PLUG
By **Paper Boi Rari**

THE STREETS MADE ME 1-3
By **Larry D. Wright**

CONFESSIONS OF A GANGSTA 1-4
CONFESSIONS OF A JACKBOY 1-3
CONFESSIONS OF A HITMAN
CONFESSIONS OF A DOPE BOY
By **Nicholas Lock**

I'M NOTHING WITHOUT HIS LOVE
SINS OF A THUG
TO THE THUG I LOVED BEFORE
A GANGSTA SAVED XMAS
IN A HUSTLER I TRUST
By **Monet Dragun**

QUIET MONEY 1-3
THUG LIFE 1-3
EXTENDED CLIP 1&2
A GANGSTA'S PARADISE
By **Trai'Quan**

CAUGHT UP IN THE LIFE 1-3
THE STREETS NEVER LET GO 1-3
By **Robert Baptiste**

NEW TO THE GAME 1-3
MONEY, MURDER & MEMORIES 1-3
By **Malik D. Rice**

CREAM 2-3
THE STREETS WILL TALK
By **Yolanda Moore**

THE STREETS WILL NEVER CLOSE 1-3
By **K'ajji**

LIFE OF A SAVAGE 1-4
A GANGSTA'S QUR'AN 1-4
MURDA SEASON 1-3
GANGLAND CARTEL 1-3
CHI'RAQ GANGSTAS 1-4
KILLERS ON ELM STREET 1-3
JACK BOYZ N DA BRONX 1-3
A DOPEBOY'S DREAM 1-3
JACK BOYS VS DOPE BOYS 1-3
COKE GIRLZ
COKE BOYS
SOSA GANG 1&2
BRONX SAVAGES
BODYMORE KINGPINS
BLOOD OF A GOON
By **Romell Tukes**

CONCRETE KILLA 1-3
VICIOUS LOYALTY 1-3
BLOODY MONEY BAGS
By **Kingpen**

THE ULTIMATE SACRIFICE 1-6
KHADIFI
IF YOU CROSS ME ONCE 1-3
ANGEL 1-4
IN THE BLINK OF AN EYE
By **Anthony Fields**

THE LIFE OF A HOOD STAR
By **Ca$h & Rashia Wilson**

NIGHTMARES OF A HUSTLA 1-3
BLOOD AND GAMES 1&2
By **King Dream**

GHOST MOB
By **Stilloan Robinson**

HARD AND RUTHLESS 1&2
MOB TOWN 251
THE BILLIONAIRE BENTLEYS 1-3
REAL G'S MOVE IN SILENCE
By **Von Diesel**

MOB TIES 1-7
SOUL OF A HUSTLER, HEART OF A KILLER 1-3
GORILLAZ IN THE TRENCHES
OOPS CRY TOO 1&2
THE DAUGHTER OF A CARTEL BOSS
By **SayNoMore**

BODYMORE MURDERLAND 1-3
THE BIRTH OF A GANGSTER 1-4
By **Delmont Player**

FOR THE LOVE OF A BOSS 1&2
By **C. D. Blue**

KILLA KOUNTY 1-5
TENDER
By **Khufu**

MOBBED UP 1-4
THE BRICK MAN 1-5
THE COCAINE PRINCESS 1-10
STEPPERS 1-3
SUPER GREMLIN 1-4
A GANGSTA'S SON
By **King Rio**

MONEY GAME 1&2
By **Smoove Dolla**

A GANGSTA'S KARMA 1-5
By **FLAME**

KING OF THE TRENCHES 1-3
By **GHOST & TRANAY ADAMS**

BAD BITCHES WIT GUNZ 1&2
PROBLEM SOLVED
By **"Christopher Diesel" Hornezes**

QUEEN OF THE ZOO 1&2
By **Black Migo**

GRIMEY WAYS 1-3
BETRAYAL OF A G
By **Ray Vinci**

XMAS WITH AN ATL SHOOTER
By **Ca$h & Destiny Skai**

KING KILLA 1&2
By **Vincent "Vitto" Holloway**

BETRAYAL OF A THUG 1&2
By **Fre$h**

COUNTDOWN OF A KILLA 1&2
SEX, MURDER AND GOD 1&2
GUNS DOWN, BOTTOMS UP 1&2
By Lo-Life

THE MURDER QUEENS 1-7
By **Michael Gallon**

FOR THE LOVE OF BLOOD 1-4
By **Jamel Mitchell**

147

FRESH OFF DA PORCH 3 | IRA B.

HOOD CONSIGLIERE 1&2
NO TIME FOR ERROR
By **Keese**

PROTÉGÉ OF A LEGEND 1,2&3
LOVE IN THE TRENCHES 1&2
By **Corey Robinson**

THE PLUG'S RUTHLESS DAUGHTER 1&2
By **Tony Daniels**

BORN IN THE GRAVE 1-3
CRIME PAYS
By **Self Made Tay**

MOAN IN MY MOUTH
By **XTASY**

TORN BETWEEN A GANGSTER AND A GENTLEMAN
By **J-BLUNT & Miss Kim**

LOYALTY IS EVERYTHING 1-3
CITY OF SMOKE 1-3
By **Molotti**

HERE TODAY GONE TOMORROW 1&2
By **Fly Rock**

WOMEN LIE MEN LIE 1-4
FIFTY SHADES OF SNOW 1-3
STACK BEFORE YOU SPLURGE
GIRLS FALL LIKE DOMINOES
NAÏVE TO THE STREETS
By **ROY MILLIGAN**

PILLOW PRINCESS
By **S. Hawkins**

148

THE BUTTERFLY MAFIA 1-3
SALUTE MY SAVAGERY 1&2
By **Fumiya Payne**

THE LANE 1&2
By Ken-Ken Spence

THE PUSSY TRAP 1-5
By **Nene Capri**

DIRTY DNA
By **Blaque**

SANCTIFIED AND HORNY
by **XTASY**

BOOKS BY LDP'S CEO, CA$H

TRUST IN NO MAN
TRUST IN NO MAN 2
TRUST IN NO MAN 3
BONDED BY BLOOD
SHORTY GOT A THUG
THUGS CRY
THUGS CRY 2
THUGS CRY 3
TRUST NO BITCH
TRUST NO BITCH 2
TRUST NO BITCH 3
TIL MY CASKET DROPS
RESTRAINING ORDER
RESTRAINING ORDER 2
IN LOVE WITH A CONVICT
LIFE OF A HOOD STAR
XMAS WITH AN ATL SHOOTER

www.ingramcontent.com/pod-product-compliance
Lightning Source LLC
Chambersburg PA
CBHW060423260626
47161CB00005B/1753